Words of Praise for

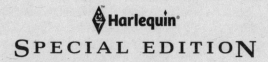

SPECIAL EDITION

from *New York Times* and *USA TODAY* bestselling authors

"When I started writing for Special Edition,
I was delighted by the length of the books,
which allowed the freedom to create,
and develop more within each character and
their romance. I have always been a fan of
Special Edition! I hope to write for it for many years
to come. Long live Special Edition!
—Diana Palmer

"My career began in Special Edition.
I remember my excitement when the SEs
were introduced, because the stories were so rich and
different, and every month when the books came out
I beat a path to the bookstore to get every one of them.
Here's to you, SE; live long, and prosper!"
—Linda Howard

"Congratulations, Special Edition,
on thirty years of publishing first-class romance!"
—Linda Lael Miller

FORTUNE'S HERO

SUSAN CROSBY

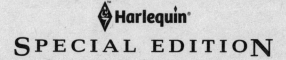

SPECIAL EDITION

ISBN-13: 978-0-373-65663-9

FORTUNE'S HERO

Copyright © 2012 by Harlequin Books S.A.

THE ANNIVERSARY PARTY
Copyright © 2012 by Harlequin Books S.A.

Recycling programs
for this product may
not exist in your area.

The publisher acknowledges the following writers who contributed to THE ANNIVERSARY PARTY: RaeAnne Thayne, Christine Rimmer, Susan Crosby, Christyne Butler, Gina Wilkins and Cindy Kirk.

www.Harlequin.com

Printed in U.S.A.

CONTENTS

Books by Susan Crosby

Harlequin Special Edition

*Husband for Hire #2118
*His Temporary Live-in Wife #2138
*Almost a Christmas Bride #2157
§§Fortune's Hero #2181

Silhouette Special Edition

*The Bachelor's Stand-In Wife #1912
††The Rancher's Surprise Marriage #1922
*The Single Dad's Virgin Wife #1930
*The Millionaire's Christmas Wife #1936
†The Pregnant Bride Wore White #1995
†Love and the Single Dad #2019
§The Doctor's Pregnant Bride? #2030
†At Long Last, a Bride #2043
‡Mendoza's Return #2102

Silhouette Desire

**Christmas Bonus, Strings Attached #1554
**Private Indiscretions #1570
**Hot Contact #1590
**Rules of Attraction #1647
**Heart of the Raven #1653
**Secrets of Paternity #1659
The Forbidden Twin #1717
Forced to the Altar #1733
Bound by the Baby #1797

Harlequin Books

Special Edition Bonus Story:
The Anniversary Party—Chapter T

**Wives for Hire
†The McCoys of Chance City
**Behind Closed Doors
††Back in Business
§The Baby Chase
‡The Fortunes of Texas:
    Lost…and Found
§§The Fortunes of Texas:
    Whirlwind Romance*

Other titles by this author
available in ebook format.

SUSAN CROSBY

believes in the value of setting goals, but also in the magic of making wishes, which often do come true—as long as she works hard enough. Along life's journey she's done a lot of the usual things—married, had children, attended college a little later than the average coed and earned a B.A. in English. Then she dove off the deep end into a full-time writing career, a wish come true.

Susan enjoys writing about people who take a chance on love, sometimes against all odds. She loves warm, strong heroes and good-hearted, self-reliant heroines, and she will always believe in happily-ever-after.

More can be learned about her at www.susancrosby.com.

Dear Reader,

Anniversary celebrations aren't just for marriages. For example, Harlequin's Special Edition line celebrates its 30th anniversary of publication this month—congratulations! And as I write this, I'm marking the anniversary of being offered my first book contract, eighteen years ago this month. Since then I've written thirty-six books. It still amazes me, every single day. The pleasure and privilege of creating a piece of work for others to read never fades.

Creating this particular book has been especially gratifying. Taking an independent Texas cowboy who's much happier among stray dogs and horses, and pairing him with a society-born much younger woman was fun and challenging. I love that Garrett Stone is clear about what he wants and doesn't want in life. Even more, I love how Victoria Fortune makes him change his very set mind.

I hope you enjoy taking their journey with them.

Susan Crosby

For Bobbie and Ernie, The Cowgirl and Her Prince.
You wrote your own romance,
and you did it so well! With love to you both.

FORTUNE'S HERO

Chapter One

"Keep away from those cowboys, they're ramblin' men…"

The lyrics to the country song popped into her head the moment she saw the tall, blue-eyed man striding past her in the terminal of the small and private, but busy, Red Rock, Texas, airport.

He caught her staring, hesitated a second, then winked. Definitely the rambling type and one to stay away from. He touched a finger to his black Stetson and just like that he was gone, the moment over.

Then the tornado hit. That black hat was the last thing she saw before the roof was ripped from above her, the roar of air sucking everything within, including her, pulling her, dragging her. Around her, wood and metal flew and crashed, ricocheted and bounced.

Pain hit first, then panic. She couldn't catch her breath, couldn't fill her lungs enough to scream. Noise. So much noise. Then suddenly no sound at all.

The quiet was almost as frightening. Gradually she heard crying, someone screaming, others calling out.

Her face was pressed against the cold concrete floor. She tried to move but couldn't. The sound of someone running toward her crept into her awareness. A man flattened himself next to her, his face in shadows—her hero, whoever he was.

"You okay?" he asked.

"My legs hurt," she managed to say, wiggling her toes and feeling them move inside her high-heeled boots, the rubble preventing leg movement.

He sprang up.

She grabbed for him, caught thin air. "Don't leave me. Please, don't—"

But he didn't leave. Weight was lifted from her, twisted metal, lumber and laminate.

"Can you drag yourself out?" he asked, this giant of a man who'd single-handedly raised the wreckage. "Hurry. There's not much time. You can do it, sweetheart. Try."

There was nothing to grab. Her useless polished fingernails dug but found no traction. She caught her breath against the unexpected pain of moving and exerted herself a little more, tried to belly crawl like a solider. Just when she thought she was going to be stuck there forever, he gripped her arm and yanked her from under the debris. Her feet cleared the mess a second before it came tumbling down. He scooped her into his strong arms and rushed away as the whole building creaked and moaned.

Panic set in. "My family…?" she asked.

He angled his head. "Over there."

She'd just started identifying relatives when part of the building they'd left crumbled with a final *whoomph*. If he'd been a minute later, she'd have been buried alive. She clenched him tighter, too shocked to say anything.

"I've got you," the stranger said. "You're safe."

The cowboy, she realized finally. The man who'd winked at her. She hadn't recognized him without his hat.

"Help will come soon," he said, his voice comforting.

She looked up as he set her down. An eerily calm sky replaced portions of the roof of the two-story structure. She'd been sitting on the other side of the room. How far had she been pulled—or thrown?

"You think you can stand on your own?" he asked.

"I think so." Her eyes were level with his chest. She focused hypnotically on the bolo tie he wore, silver and onyx, before looking up at him.

"You'll be okay," he said, releasing her, understanding in his eyes.

Before he could abandon her, she grabbed him

by his bolo and tugged him down for a quick, hard, thank-you-for-saving-me kiss, over as soon as it started. Her heart lodged in her throat, damming up the words trapped inside. She couldn't even ask his name—or tell him hers.

He cupped her shoulders and moved back. For an instant his eyes met hers, then he was running away from her. Paralyzed, she didn't budge for a minute, then she finally focused on her surroundings. It looked like a war zone. Some of her family were sitting in shock; some were running around. Suitcases were scattered everywhere. What had once been a small plane lay nose-down not twenty feet from where she'd been sitting before the tornado hit.

When she turned back to the terminal she saw no sign of the cowboy. Transfixed, she moved toward the luggage, thinking to stack it all together, needing something to do. Then she heard sirens approach and she staggered toward the sound, waving—

Victoria Fortune jerked awake, sweating, her sheets tangled, her long, dark hair stuck to her skin. She'd had the dream again, the same vivid but increasingly detailed dream. The tornado had struck on December 30 in Red Rock, Texas. She'd been headed home after being a bridesmaid in her cousin Wendy's wedding. Now, three months later, Victoria was safe in her own bed, in her own condo, in her hometown of Atlanta, Georgia. Three months, and she was still dreaming about it.

And *him*. She didn't even know his name, never

even thanked him, the man who could've died with her that day but who'd rescued her without regard to his own safety.

She was sick of it, physically ill from the constant nightmares and loss of sleep. Even during the day she was assaulted by visions of the destruction and the surreal feel of the tornado sweeping her across the floor.

Maybe it'd been even worse this time because she'd talked to her cousin Jordana last night, who'd suffered her own traumas, and they'd agreed Victoria should go to Red Rock so they could deal with their problems together. Support each other. Be there for each other.

Victoria glanced at the clock then threw off the covers, realizing she needed to start packing for her late-morning flight. She was going to face the past and deal with her near-death experience. She also needed to thank her hero, which was long overdue.

But first she called her parents to tell them she wouldn't be attending the requisite family Sunday brunch.

"The pew was mostly empty this morning," her father, James Marshall Fortune, said when he answered the phone.

"I'm sorry, Daddy. I overslept."

"You party too much," he said gruffly but softly. As the youngest child and only daughter, Victoria got away with more than her four brothers could. Occasionally she used that to her advantage.

"What constitutes 'too much'?" Victoria asked

sweetly, making an effort with her beloved father. Even he had been openly worried about her.

"Ha! We'll wait for you. Your brothers aren't all here yet, either. Only Shane."

Victoria wandered onto the balcony off her bedroom. She was on the fifteenth floor. "I'm not coming at all, Daddy. I'm heading to Red Rock in a couple of hours."

"I thought you'd decided to skip that party."

"I did skip it. The party was last night, but Jordana and Emily are still at Wendy's house. We're going to have a little girl time, just us four cousins. Well, plus Wendy's new husband and baby. Please tell Shane I'm taking a few days of vacation, all right?"

"Your brother is your boss. If you need time off, you need to square it with him yourself. And I'm sure your mother will have something to say."

"Yes, sir." Her father made it sound like she was a sixteen-year-old kid instead of a twenty-four-year-old college graduate who lived alone and held down a good job—if she could hold on to it. She hadn't been pulling her own weight for a while now.

"Shane overheard and says that's good news," her mother said, coming onto the line. "What's going on, honey?"

Victoria repeated what she'd said to her father.

"You're still having bad dreams," her mother said.

"Yes, ma'am. They're not going away on their own."

"What about that man—that cowboy who rescued you? Are you going to see him?"

"I need to thank him. It's been haunting me that I haven't. I think that's part of my problem."

"I can see where it could help. Are you taking the company jet?"

Victoria closed her eyes. "I'd have to land at Red Rock Airport, and I'm not ready for that. I'll fly into San Antonio and rent a car."

"Call me if you need me. I think it's good you're doing this, sugar. Important. You've looked so tired."

"Thanks, Mom." But it was more than *good,* Victoria thought. It was necessary. She hadn't been able to deal with molehills lately, much less mountains.

Hours later she drove into downtown Red Rock, then pulled up in front of Marcos and Wendy Mendoza's pretty three-bedroom house. Wendy had been working her magic on the place, transforming it from bachelor pad to family home, a fun mix of contemporary and cottage styles. She'd been gardening, too, Victoria could tell. What had been barren at the time of the wedding in December now bloomed with welcoming spring beauty.

Wendy burst onto the front porch. At twenty-two, she was two years younger than Victoria, and she sported the same long brown hair and eyes. She was more openly bubbly than Victoria, but as first cousins, they'd been as close as sisters. So were Jordana and Emily, Wendy's sisters.

"Where's the star of this show?" Victoria asked, hugging Wendy.

"Sleeping. Finally," Wendy answered. "Marcos is working."

"And your sisters?" Victoria asked as they stepped into the house.

"Emily went for a walk. Jordana left."

Victoria stopped. "She left? When? Why? I talked to her just last night. She said she would wait for me."

"I don't know what happened. She took off right after lunch. Honestly, Vicki, Jordana was acting weird the whole time she was here. Em noticed it, too. We're worried about her. Did she tell you what's going on?"

She had, but Victoria couldn't tell Jordana's secrets. Victoria made a noncommittal sound as she checked her cell phone for messages, finding none from Jordana.

"You can bunk with Em instead of at the hotel now that Jordana's gone. Would you like some tea?" Wendy asked. "We could sit on the sunporch for a while."

"Yes, fine," Victoria said, trying to drum up some enthusiasm for Wendy's sake.

"Meet you on the porch in a minute." She laid a hand on Victoria's arm. "Are you all right?"

"I'm fine. Just fine. Why is everyone asking me that?" She closed her eyes and gritted her teeth. "I'm sorry, Wendy. I really am. I don't know if I'm all right. I know I haven't been myself. I'm hoping this trip will be the vacation I need."

Victoria carried her suitcase into the guest room. How could Jordana leave without a word to her? They needed each other.

And she needed the name of her rescuer. Needed to see him, thank him. She wasn't in the mood for idle chitchat, but she knew good manners indicated she should spend time with her hostess first.

Victoria peeked into the baby's room, caught a glimpse of a tiny pink bundle in the bassinet, then tiptoed out, afraid of waking six-week-old Mary-Anne.

"I'm surprised that Emily is still here," Victoria said to Wendy as they sat in the glassed-in sunporch. "She's been staying with you for weeks. How long can she stay away from work?"

"I've stopped asking her that question. I figure she knows what she's doing. She's been a huge help since we brought MaryAnne home. She was so tiny, you know, as premature as she was, but so perfect. Emily's a natural mom. She steadied me." Wendy looked around. "Honestly, though, I think Marcos is looking forward to the three of us becoming a family on our own."

Victoria sat up straight. "Of course he wants that. You must, too." Just like all she wanted was to talk to the stranger who'd saved her. "I'll encourage Em to go home, and I'll move to the hotel. We're being so—"

"Stop. Please, Vicki, I didn't mean right this

second. Marcos is glad I've had company since he works such long hours at the restaurant. I just meant that I think we're both ready to establish our own routine. But not this week. Not yet."

"Well, I only plan to stay a few days. I'll get Em to leave with me, too."

"It's not necessary, Vicki. Really. I think she's hiding out here, but I'm not sure why. And then there's Jordana—"

"Who is the biggest mystery of all," Emily said, coming into the room. She was tall, blonde and green-eyed, yet she also had the Fortune look about her. "Hey, Vicki." She bent to give her cousin a hug while eyeing Wendy. "I'm not hiding out here, sister mine. I've been helping. I've also been working from here. You look like crap, Vicki."

"Thank you so much."

Emily shrugged. "Is MaryAnne still sleeping?"

"Like a baby," Wendy said with a grin.

The women settled into conversation, as they had all their lives. Their fathers were brothers, highly successful, self-made financial geniuses in Atlanta, each owning separate companies that weren't in competition with each other. It was amazing, actually, that the cousins got along so well, considering that their fathers did not. At family events, the brothers ignored each other. Only the two men knew what was behind their estrangement.

"So, Vicki," Emily said, "why did you come today instead of in time for the party last night?"

Because my sanity depended on it. "Jordana and

I talked last night, and it just seemed like the right time."

"Did she tell you what's going on with her?"

"Going on?" Victoria asked innocently.

Wendy and Emily exchanged glances. "She doesn't look well," Emily said. "In fact, she looks worse than you. We're really worried."

"I think she's fine," Victoria answered. "She's dealing with some stuff. No, don't ask. She's not sick. Wendy," she said, changing the subject. She couldn't wait a second longer. "Did Marcos ever figure out who got me out from under the debris? I would like to talk to him."

"He's pretty sure it must have been Garrett Stone."

Garrett Stone. Her heart skipped a beat or two. She finally had a name to put to him, a strong name, solid. Heroic. "Where does he live?"

"He's got a ranch—although I'm using the term loosely—outside town called Pete's Retreat. He's born-and-bred Red Rock, but he's left town a couple of times, for several years at a time. There've been rumors about him, apparently."

"Like what?"

"For one thing, he was involved in some kind of scandal years ago with a young woman. That forced him to leave town the first time. For another, no one knows how he makes a living. Plus he's a loner. He's got dogs and a few horses. Strays gravitate to him."

Victoria remembered he was a man of few words, and also how his hands had been gentle on her.

Now that she was here, she wanted to get it over with. To see him. To thank him. To take back her life. "Could you give me directions to his place? I'd like to go there now."

"I can call Marcos and ask," Wendy said. "But I think it would be better if one of us went with you."

"Why?"

"In case he's rude or something."

"Standing-on-the-porch-holding-a-shotgun rude or just brusque? He can't be totally without civility. He saved my life, after all. And besides, I'm not without charm, you know," she added, fluttering her eyelashes.

"I doubt anything in your past has prepared you for Garrett Stone," Wendy said. "Face it, Vicki, the easy appeal you have comes from having led a charmed life. We all have. If you're expecting him to welcome you with open arms and listen to you shower him with gratitude, you're deluded. I gather people don't venture out to his ranch. There must be a reason for that. I'm not sure he'll be nice to you."

"I'm not a princess," Victoria said, crossing her arms. "If he doesn't want to hear what I have to say, so be it. At least I will have done what I need to."

"Wow. You've really gotten snippy."

Victoria dug for patience. "I'm sorry for my attitude. It's just been weighing on me."

"I see that. What I think is that you've got a big ol' case of hero worship, some big fantasy you've worked up in your head about him without knowing the whole truth," Emily said. "And although we may not wear crowns, we Fortune daughters have been protected and pampered since birth. You can't deny that. But the men of Red Rock are different from the men in our social circle back home."

"Meaning what?"

"Have you ever been rejected, Vicki?"

"Of course I have. But it's not like this is a love connection, you know. I just have a few things to say." Except that she'd been fantasizing about him, too, that he'd carried her far away, her hero.

Emily raised her hands in surrender. "Okay, then. At least you'll know what to expect if you go there."

Victoria frowned, thinking it over. She *had* been rejected. Maybe not by anyone who mattered, but then she'd never been in love, either. Perhaps because she'd never developed any long-term relationships, something that had irked her parents to no end. As old-fashioned as the notion was, she'd been expected to find a future husband while she was in college. Her parents were old-school, with traditional expectations, and she hadn't lived up to them. It was different for her four older brothers, who were still single, their martial status not even an issue.

Armed with directions from Marcos, Victoria headed out twenty minutes later. She'd brought a bottle of eighteen-year-old single-malt, award-winning Scotch whiskey. She'd never tasted it herself, preferring sweet, fruity drinks, but the whiskey was praised by most men she knew.

It wasn't a long drive, but an increasingly desolate one. Why anyone would want to live so far from civilization puzzled her. She liked her creature comforts, which meant shops and restaurants within walking distance and the theater and opera close enough to attend frequently. It was the reason why she lived in a condo in downtown Atlanta. She loved the action.

Finally she saw the mailbox Marcos had told her to watch for. She turned into the property. There was no sign announcing she'd arrived at Pete's Retreat, no welcoming fence-lined driveway, just a long dirt path. After a minute, she spotted a corral with three horses, then some dogs began to bark, several rushing up to her car. She slowed way down, afraid of accidentally hitting one. Garrett Stone may take in strays, but he sure didn't train them well. Or maybe he wasn't home to call them off—

No. There he was, coming from a barn. Strolling, actually. Or maybe moseying, that slim-hipped stride she associated with cowboys, no-nonsense and no-hurry at the same time. He was as tall as she remembered, a foot taller than she, and she was five-four.

She stopped the car in front of his house, an old but well-maintained, single-story ranch style. He came to a halt in front of her vehicle and stared at her through the windshield, apparently not recognizing her. He still hadn't called off the dogs, who barked and jumped. She felt imprisoned in her car.

Finally he made a motion with his hand and the dogs dropped to all fours and stopped barking. They sidled closer to him. With another hand motion, all but two dogs headed toward a barn.

Victoria opened the window and called out, "Hi! You probably don't remember me. I'm Victoria Fortune. From the airport? The tornado?"

"I remember." His face was shadowed by his hat, so she couldn't judge his reaction, except she thought he was frowning.

"Will your dogs attack me if I get out of the car?"

"Probably not."

She expected him to wink, as he had at the airport, but his expression never changed, no sign to indicate whether or not he was joking. Even though she felt unsure of her welcome, she grabbed her gift and opened the door. When the dogs didn't growl, she climbed out, grateful she'd changed into jeans and boots so that she fit in better. Still he didn't move.

"I was in the neighborhood…" she began. Nervous now, she brushed at some dust on her jeans, giving herself something to do, wishing he would pick up the conversation.

His mouth quirked, but whether it was a sign of annoyance or humor, she didn't know.

She thrust the whiskey at him, apparently a little too hard. It hit him in the stomach and bounced off obviously strong abs. He grabbed for the container. The bottle fell—

He caught it at his knees.

"Whew!" she said, grinning. "Good catch."

He eyed the container. If he knew how expensive

it was, he didn't indicate it; he just waited for her to speak. Or leave, she guessed.

"Maybe we could go inside?" she asked.

"Why?" he asked.

"I—I'd like to talk to you."

"Here's as good a place as any. You're interrupting my work."

"What do you do?"

"This 'n that."

She crossed her arms. He might look exactly like the man from the airport, but he no longer seemed like the winking type. "You're loving this, aren't you?"

"What?"

"Being the taciturn cowboy. Keeping the myth alive."

"Taciturn. That's a mighty big word, ma'am."

Aha! There *was* a glimmer in his gorgeous blue eyes. He was just playing with her. He'd probably decided she was just another pretty face. "Something tells me you know its definition, but okay. You win. I came here to thank you for saving my life."

"You told me three months ago."

"No, I didn't."

"You kissed me. Pretty much said it all. Can't say it was the best kiss I've ever had planted on me, but I got what you were meaning by it."

She narrowed her eyes. "If I'd wanted to kiss you in a memorable way, I would've, but I guarantee you I put more emotion into that one kiss than any other I've given."

"Well, isn't that a sorry state of affairs."

"I'm a good kisser!"

"If you say so, ma'am." He touched the brim of his hat. "Have a safe drive back to town." He walked away from her.

She called out, "You know, cowboy, where I come from, it's rude to walk out on a visitor."

"Where I come from, princess," he said over his shoulder, "it's rude to drop in uninvited."

Chapter Two

Garrett didn't slow his stride. His old hound Pete trotted beside him and kept looking back at the woman who'd audibly gasped her indignation at his abrupt dismissal. Truth was, she tempted him mightily, and he was afraid if he invited her in, even for just a second, he would fall under her spell. It was obvious that she was trouble with a capital *T*.

The moment he'd caught sight of her at the airport three months ago, he'd felt gut punched. A few seconds later he'd recovered enough to wink at her, but had kept walking because he'd been inclined to start up a conversation, which would've been a big mistake. She wasn't his type at all, which had made it all the more baffling. Two birthdays from now he would turn forty. She looked barely out of college.

She was petite and dark-haired, and he was partial to blonde and tall, or at least closer to his own six foot four than she was. She wore designer-chic clothes, even her jeans and boots had probably come from a boutique or something, and she'd already turned up her nose at the good Texas dust that had settled on her jeans as if she'd been contaminated.

He'd met plenty of high-maintenance women in his life. He'd learned to avoid them, especially after an experience a couple of years back with a woman named Crystal, one he'd like to forget, except for the lesson learned.

But he also liked women with curves. Give him more than a handful of a woman in his big bed and he was happy, especially if she was just passing through. He didn't date women looking for long-term, and felt no need for conversation or companionship on a regular basis.

Sure, the petite Ms. Victoria Fortune of the Atlanta Fortunes was wife material—but not for him. She'd had stars in her eyes when she'd arrived a few minutes ago. He wasn't sure what had caused them. Glorification of him as her hero, maybe? He'd never been a hero in anyone's eyes before. Just the opposite, in fact. He'd been blamed for lots he didn't do, just because people expected it.

He'd been a rabble-rouser in his youth, prone to bar fights and speeding tickets, but that'd been years ago. And then there was that incident with Jenny Kirkpatrick....

It hadn't mattered that he'd been a teenager at the

time—nor had he been the guilty party. Some reputations couldn't be lived down, however, so he'd stopped trying.

Pete assumed his usual dog-sentinel post on the porch as Garrett let himself into his house. He decided to wait until Victoria was gone before resuming his work. When he didn't hear her car start up, he set down the bottle of fine whiskey, peeked out a window and saw her leaning against her car, arms crossed, staring his direction. His collie-mix mutt, Abel, plopped next to her, his tail wagging, dust flying. Idly she petted him, then crouched and gave him a good scratch behind his ears, something Abel loved more than anything except a good belly rub. What male didn't?

Picturing her hands sliding over his own body knotted him up good—and how the hell long was she gonna hang around when he'd specifically dismissed her?

Everyone knew Fortune women liked their luxuries, and they probably always got their way, too. Maybe she wouldn't leave until he forced her off his property.

Well, she wouldn't get her way here. Not with him.

Choking off a colorful oath, he opened his front door, jammed on his hat and strode across his yard. Abel stood and wagged his tail, looking a little guilty at being caught getting attention from another human.

And *that* human was looking at him like he was a rock star or something. Aw, hell.

"Why are you still here?" he asked.

"I'm not a princess," she said calmly. "I came here because I dream about you every night."

Gut punched again, he said nothing. He'd had a few dreams himself....

"Nightmares, really," she added.

So much for hero worship. "You need professional help with that. You're not gonna find that here."

"I'm sure you're right. But I've never been that close to death, Mr. Stone. So I decided to come see you, to thank you, with the hope that I can stop thinking about it, obsessing about it really. I would appreciate it if you would acknowledge the fact you saved my life and let me thank you properly for doing so. I'm sure I'll be able to move on then."

"And just how long does it take to say thank you?"

She cocked her head. "How long does it take to pour a glass of whiskey?"

She had sass, he gave her that. Sometimes that was a good quality in a woman.

"Are you of legal drinking age?"

"I'm twenty-four."

"Are you expected back right away?" he asked.

"I suppose my family will worry after a little while. Why?"

"Before we break open that whiskey, we need to go for a drive."

"Where?" she asked, a touch of suspicion in her voice.

He angled closer. "Well, now, if you don't trust me..."

Her eyes shimmered, eyes the color of chocolate diamonds and just as deep. "Let's just say my entire family knows I'm here, so I don't think trust is an issue," she said.

"C'mon, then." He crossed the yard to where his pickup sat, he could hear her boots crunching against the hard ground. He got into his truck, expecting she would climb in the passenger side on her own, since she wasn't a princess. He smiled a little at that.

"Buckle up," he said when she settled next to him.

They made the trip in silence, and he could feel her tension rise with every mile. Then when he made the last turn into Red Rock Airport, her fingers dug into the seat. Her eyes were glued on the structures ahead as he paused.

He sat still, letting her take in the view, letting her adjust to seeing the place where she'd almost been buried alive. Seeing the airport rebuilt should help her rebuild her own life.

"Let's go inside," he said, keeping his voice soft and low, treating her the same as any wounded animal who'd landed on his property.

She nodded. He admired her for that, for not making him coax her, for facing her demons. He came around the truck as she dropped onto the ground, then he walked toward the terminal. She caught up with him in a couple of seconds and gripped his hand, keeping up with him.

"The airport's back to being used all the time," he said. "They're close to finishing the rebuilding."

"How many people died?" she asked.

"Three." He eyed her. "Could've been a whole lot worse."

"What were you doing here?"

"Picking up a shipment that'd been airfreighted to me." He opened the glass door to the terminal and took her inside with him. She squeezed his hand tighter, if that was even possible. "Clear skies, Victoria. Don't worry."

"Hey, Garrett!"

"Boyd," Garrett said, acknowledging the jack-of-all-trades airport worker he'd known since grade school.

"Need somethin'?"

"I'm showing off the construction."

Boyd waved a hand then walked away.

"It's just a building," Garrett said, feeling her start to shake.

"It was almost my tomb."

His, too, but he didn't remind her of that. He'd been able to tuck it away in his memories.

It was dark by the time they'd walked the entire place. She never let go of his hand, and he had to admit it was kinda nice holding it. Every now and then he noticed the sparkle of her nail polish, felt the softness of her skin against his rough hand and how small it was compared to his—all indicators of how different they were.

She was just as quiet on the drive back to his ranch. He hadn't expected a miraculous recovery for her, but he'd thought maybe she would chat him up a bit. She petted Pete and Abel after she climbed out of his truck, crooning to them. Garrett wouldn't admit to being jealous, but he felt…something.

"You still want that whiskey?" he asked.

She looked up at him. Her smile was calmer than when she'd first arrived. "Rain check?"

He didn't answer because he didn't expect to see her again. He walked her to her car, opened her door and waited for her to get inside and go. He was in a hurry for her to leave him in peace. He'd thought he'd buried his own memories, but being at the airport with her had brought them back in full. He could toss six feet of dirt over them again, but he needed quiet to do that. And for Ms. Victoria Fortune to be out of his sight.

"Thank you," she said, a little quaver to her voice.

Aw, hell. She wasn't gonna cry, was she? *That* he couldn't deal with at all. "You drive safe now."

She was staring at him, at his chest anyway. "You were wearing a bolo tie that day," she said. "Silver and onyx. It was gorgeous."

What he remembered was how she'd grabbed his tie and pulled him down to kiss him. He also remembered her perfume, sweet and spicy. She didn't wear any today, and he liked that, too.

Finally she raised her gaze to connect with his, searching his eyes.

"Thank you for taking me there." Then, surprising him, she reached up, locked her arms behind his neck and tugged him down as she raised up on tiptoe. He could've easily set her aside. Instead, he met her halfway and accepted her final gesture of appreciation. Her lips were soft, her mouth hot. When she tightened her hold on him, he did the same, pulling her body next to his, wrapping his arms around her, sliding his hands down to cup her rear.

Then Abel jumped up on him from behind and her cell phone rang at the same time, a double jolt of awareness to the situation they'd been about to put themselves in.

"I'd better answer that," she said, stepping back to dig into her pocket, her hands shaking. "Someone's probably worried."

He backed off as she took the call, telling the person on the other end that she was on her way home. Then she tucked her phone away. He had no idea what to say, so he left it to her because his next move would be to haul her to bed.

"I should go," she said. She climbed into her car and started the engine. Her smile turned mischievous, the dull glaze in her eyes replaced with more clarity. "I didn't want you to think I wasn't a good kisser," she said pertly, then she gave him an indecipherable look through the windshield as she backed up to turn around. She waved as she drove off.

His body was like granite. He hadn't been this on edge for a long time. He was usually the one with the last word, too. She'd caught him off guard. That was also rare.

Maybe he'd helped her with her post-tornado trauma, but she'd given him something to dream about.

It was the last thing he wanted.

Red Rock's most upscale restaurant, Red, was situated in the heart of downtown. Wendy's husband, Marcos Mendoza, managed the restaurant that was owned by his aunt and uncle. It was where Marcos and Wendy had met. She'd been exiled, as she referred to it, from the family business in Atlanta and sent to Red Rock to work for one of the Fortune businesses to discover her talent. She eventually ended up at Red, first as a waitress, then finding her calling as a dessert chef.

The original building was a converted, very old hacienda rumored to have belonged to relatives of the infamous General Santa Anna. It had been rebuilt after a fire but still featured an inside courtyard with a water fountain and several dining areas, both public and private.

Stepping into the main dining room, Victoria admired the rich, colorful decor and peaceful aura. Wendy had urged her and Emily to get out of the house for a while, and Marcos had insisted they have a spectacular dessert on him at Red. They'd argued it was unnecessary, but Wendy had prevailed. She couldn't take MaryAnne out in public for at least two more weeks, according to the pediatrician. She would go to bed when the baby did, and she wanted Emily and Victoria to have some fun.

They sat at the bar, where they had a good view of the restaurant that was a little too understated to be called a "fun" spot. It was a place to gather or go on a date, but not a mix-and-mingle hot spot, nor was there a dance floor in the main room.

"So," Emily said after taking a taste of a creamy dessert called Heavenly Sin and licking her spoon clean. "You've been awfully quiet since you got back from seeing Garrett Stone."

Victoria took a bite of a black-and-white pudding that melted in her mouth. She closed her eyes, savoring it before she spoke. "There's not much to say. I thanked him. He decided I needed to see the airport and took me there, as some kind of therapy, I expect."

"Was he right? Did it help?"

"I suppose I'll find out tonight. If the dream doesn't return, I'll call it a success."

"And was the cowboy rough around the edges or gorgeous?"

"Both."

Emily's brows went up. "Do tell."

"He's different" was all she said.

He came across as a man who didn't rile easily, was in fact paternal and protective, but he also simmered with passion. He just kept a tight rein on it. She could tell when he'd been restraining himself.

That kind of self-control, Victoria thought, was even sexier. And it made her want to break through it.

She dipped her spoon into the pudding again just as the cowboy in question took a seat at the bar, not close enough to talk to, but close enough to exchange glances. The bartender drew a draft and set it in front of Garrett without any words being spoken. He lifted his glass toward Victoria, took a sip and looked away.

"You're blushing," Emily said then looked around, her gaze landing on Garrett, who steadfastly stared at the wall of bottles behind the bartender. "Is that *him?*" Emily whispered.

"Who?"

Emily gave her a tolerant look. "Your therapist."

"Yes. And don't you dare put him on your Baby Plan list."

Emily turned again and caught him studying them. "He'd make great babies, don't you think? Tall and lean, and those ooh-la-la blue eyes."

"Off-limits," Victoria said, feeling her face heat up even more. "Anyway, I thought you were looking to adopt. At least that was your plan a week ago."

"That was originally my goal, but looking at Cowboy Freud here, I don't know…." She grinned. "Don't fret, Vicki. I can see you've got the hots for him. I won't unleash my considerable charms on your man."

"He's not my man." She scraped her bowl for the last taste of pudding.

"Yet."

"I'll be going home in a couple of days."

"I didn't hear you say you weren't attracted."

Victoria shrugged. Attracted? What a mild word…

Garrett stood then and moved to sit next to Emily. They made a beautiful couple. She was several inches taller than Victoria. Her blond hair was more golden than his darker blond, but they fit together.

So much for his being a loner. She tried to remember why she'd labeled him that in her mind.

"Evenin', Ms. Fortune," he said, looking at Victoria.

"Hello, Mr. Stone." The fact they'd shared a passionate kiss and were being so formal with each other made her heart beat faster, as if she was hiding something, when usually her life was an open book. She introduced him to her cousin.

"You following me?" he asked Victoria over the rim of his glass.

She arched her brows. "I believe we were sitting right here when you arrived," she said, pointing out the obvious, not appreciating Emily's curious and rather amused expression.

"Everyone knows I'm here every Sunday night 'round this time."

"I'm new in town. No one thought to add me to the Garrett Stone Sunday Routine loop."

Marcos came up to them and shook Garrett's hand, welcoming him. No, she hadn't known, but

Marcos certainly must have, and he'd issued the command performance to come to Red tonight. Why?

"Were Em's and my desserts Wendy's creations? Is that why you insisted we come tonight?" Victoria asked Marcos, making sure that Garrett knew exactly who was responsible for her being at Red tonight.

"Only the flan recipe on the dessert menu isn't hers, although she's talking about creating a chocolate version."

A server put a plate of enchiladas in front of Garrett, smiled flirtatiously at him—or maybe *knowingly*—then sauntered away. Marcos excused himself, then Emily stood.

"I'll be back in a few minutes," she said.

Victoria was glad for the empty seat between her and Garrett because she wanted too much to sit closer, to brush arms, to straddle him right where he sat. "So, you come in every Sunday night for enchiladas?"

"And to pick up a standing order for a week's worth of dinners."

"You don't cook, I guess."

"I barbecue now and then, and breakfast and lunch are easy, but dinner's a challenge. They freeze individual portions for me. Makes it simple."

"You don't get tired of eating the same things night after night?"

"Nope." He scooped up a mixture of rice and beans then chewed thoughtfully while watching her. After he swallowed, he said, "You okay after today?"

"So far, so good." She couldn't remember being this tempted by a man. She'd had plenty of flirtations in her life, but she craved Garrett. He'd dominated her dreams for months, had held her hand for an hour, kissed her once—but very well—and now he was just sitting there, eating, and she wanted to go home with him.

He eyed her. "Your cheeks are pink."

"It's warm in here."

"You sure you're just not remembering our kiss?"

She angled her body toward him and crossed her legs, pleased that the kiss was on his mind, too. "I told you I was a good kisser."

"It takes two."

She smiled leisurely. "It certainly does."

He gave her a cool look, which made her laugh.

"When do you go back to Atlanta?" he asked.

"Soon. I don't want to overstay my welcome." She leaned closer. "I'd like to see you again."

"Why?" He didn't seem surprised, which annoyed her.

"You interest me," she said.

"And you usually get what you want, I expect."

She thought she should be offended by that, but realized he was speaking the truth as he saw it. She was a Fortune, therefore her life must never hit any speed bumps.

"Most of the time I guess I do," she answered,

although she'd never wanted anything that mattered a whole lot—until now.

He stood, tossed a couple of bills down for the bartender, then swiped his hat off the bar top. Was he going to take off without another word?

"May I come out to your place tomorrow?" she asked, her insides churning. He apparently didn't have a high opinion of her. She'd like the opportunity to change that.

"Not a good idea."

Her brows went up. "That wasn't a no."

He touched a finger to her chin, then dragged it down her neck, his expression intense. "It sure as hell wasn't a yes. Good night, princess."

"See you around, cowboy," she replied, pleased her voice didn't shake.

She watched him walk away and sighed. The skin he'd touched still burned. She'd always wondered what it would be like to want a man like that, really want him. Now she knew.

It probably wasn't smart on her part, trying to get him to meet with her again and see what happened, but an insistent voice in her head—and heart—was telling her to pursue him. She'd always been the resistant one, the person to keep a suitor at arm's length. Now the tables were turned, and she totally understood the frustration of being rejected, or at least being held off.

She wasn't proud of her past behavior, but in her own defense, she hadn't understood it, either.

Emily returned. They put on their jackets and walked back to the Mendoza house.

"You looked like you wanted to gobble that man up," Emily said.

"Too bad he wasn't on the menu," Victoria said, smiling, enjoying the crisp April evening. Life was so different here from Atlanta, so starkly different. "Wendy seems to love living here, Em. I never would've predicted that."

"I'm not sure it's the *where* but the *who*. She loves Marcos. That's all that matters to her. Plus she found a passion for making desserts, so now she has a career. Add in motherhood..." Her voice trailed off. She shrugged.

"Are you envious?" Victoria asked. "I know how much you want to be a mother. It would be good to have a husband first."

"In an ideal world. How about you? Unlike me, you've never talked about—"

"Obsessed about, you mean," Victoria interrupted.

Emily nodded. "I admit to an obsession. Anyway, you've never said anything about wanting a family."

"I've given it some thought, but I'm not in a hurry. I don't think I've found *me* yet. I've got a job that doesn't excite me, but I don't know what else I want to do. I have great friends, but they're settling into relationships and careers, so I feel at a loss a lot of the time. I've gotten restless."

As they left the downtown, the night seemed darker and quieter, and yet Victoria felt safe. She didn't know how safe she would feel at Pete's Retreat. Garrett's desolate location, where animals and humans could be hovering without anyone knowing, made her nervous. What a city girl she was.

Victoria's cell rang just as they reached the house. Emily went inside, leaving Victoria alone on the porch.

"Coward," Victoria said into the phone instead of hello.

"No question about it," her cousin Jordana said. "I'm sorry. I just couldn't stay any longer. Couldn't do what I said I would."

"Your sisters are worried about you. They think you're seriously ill."

"What did you tell them?"

"That they shouldn't worry, because you're not. But you know you'll be showing soon. How long do you expect to keep your secret?"

"I already can't fasten some of my pants."

"Then you can't delay. And Jordana? Tanner deserves to know."

"Soon," she said. "I'm not ready. How about you? Did you meet your rescuer?"

"I did." She told her cousin about her visit with Garrett, although not about the kiss. "As soon as I get home, we'll talk."

"When you were at the airport, did you…"

"See Tanner?" Victoria said, finishing her question. "No. But it's Sunday, and the flight school probably isn't open on Sunday. The building looks pretty much done. It was hard for me to tell without going inside."

After they ended their conversation, Victoria sat on the porch steps. The air felt cooler now that she wasn't moving, but she didn't seek the warmth of the house yet. She set her arms on her knees and rested her chin there, her eyes closed. It'd been a long day, but she needed to examine it, needed to decide if she was truly taken with Garrett or the *idea* of him—what she'd built up in her mind. That he'd added to his list of heroic qualities by taking her to the airport deepened her need to see him again.

It wasn't like her to fall so quickly and so hard. Maybe his resistance had presented her with a challenge, and she didn't have many challenges in her life these days. It was exhilarating. She felt anxious for night to come so the next day could start. It'd been months since that had happened. Maybe longer than that.

Without question, she had to see him again. She couldn't go home with her mind full of him. It would be worse than the nightmares from the tornado. At least those were limited to nighttime. Garrett would haunt her daytime hours, too.

She stood then, her decision made. She would figure out a way to see him again, somehow let him see the real Victoria—at least the one she wanted to become because of him.

Chapter Three

"She's fourteen years younger than me," Garrett said the next morning to his hound as he followed along to the next stall. "Plus she was born with a silver spoon in her mouth. And she's...she's short."

Pete wagged his tail, the dog equivalent of "I hear you, man."

Garrett tossed used straw into a wheelbarrow. "On the other hand, she *is* just passing through. That's a good thing, right?"

Pete cocked his head and whined a little.

"I get it. She's the marrying kind. I need to re-member that."

Pete looked away then took off running at the same moment Garrett heard a car coming down his driveway. The rest of the dogs followed. It was probably the straw he'd ordered earlier being delivered. At least he hoped so.

No such luck. He spotted Victoria's car. She tapped the horn twice and the dogs scattered except Pete and Abel. Pete stopped when Garrett did. Abel hurried over to greet her. Garrett didn't call him off.

"Well, don't you look all spiffy," she said, grinning. "Those rubber boots are the height of fashion." She was wearing the same thing she'd worn yesterday, except her shirt was deep purple, low cut and a little frilly. Garrett had a soft spot for feminine frills, even more if they were red, lacy and barely covering a fine female body. He wondered what she was wearing underneath…

"I've been muckin' manure, princess. Wanna help?"

She wrinkled her nose. "Maybe another time."

"Uh-huh."

She made the mistake of stopping downwind of him. After a second, she waved her hand in front of her face. "You weren't kidding."

"You take your chances when you come uninvited." He cupped her arms and reversed their positions.

"I thought you'd like to know that I didn't have the nightmare last night," she said.

He'd had one. It'd been a hell of a night, in fact. "Good. So, now you've come to say goodbye?"

Her eyes sparkled. "Did you think I'd let you off that easily, cowboy?"

"Meaning?"

"I still want to get to know you."

The last thing he wanted was more alone time with her. He turned on his heel and headed back to the barn. "You're welcome to watch me work."

He heard her following him and shook his head. She was like a mosquito. A stubborn, tenacious… and damned sexy pest.

He'd reached the barn door when the sound of a truck stopped him. His order of straw. Great. Lenny, the delivery driver, would spot Victoria and the town would soon be alive with rumor. Hell.

"You look like you want me to hide," Victoria said. "You don't want anyone to know I'm here, I suppose?"

Her insight surprised him. "*Would* you hide?"

"Heck no." She laughed.

He eyed her steadily, resettled his hat on his head and went to greet Lenny, a sixty-year-old man who only seemed slow. He backed his truck to the barn door, hopped down and lumbered to where Garrett stood, waiting, Victoria next to him.

"Howdy, Garrett." Lenny grabbed a bale hook, as did Garrett.

They worked in silence until the bales were unloaded and stacked. Garrett didn't order too much at a time, preferring fresh straw and feed. His barn wasn't huge, just ten stalls, one where he stored straw and another a tack room. Plus his workshop, hidden from casual glances.

When Garrett didn't introduce Victoria, Lenny

made it a point to do the honors. He lifted his gimme cap for a second. "Lenny Paulson, miss."

"I'm Victoria Fortune." She extended her hand as if he'd just washed up for supper, when in fact he was a mess from head to toe.

He hesitated, looked at his hand, then grasped hers for less than a second. "You Fortunes seem to have populated the whole earth."

She laughed. "We have many branches all over the country, that's for sure, and most have been fruitful. I have four brothers myself in Atlanta."

"Whacha doin' with this reprobate?"

"Learning how to muck stalls."

Garrett almost laughed. She'd said it with a straight face.

"That so?" Lenny asked. "Got much call to do that in Hotlanta, do you?"

"You might be surprised."

Lenny guffawed. He pulled a folded piece of paper from his back pocket and passed it, along with a pencil stub, to Garrett, who signed the bill.

"He ain't much of a bargain," Lenny said to Victoria as he headed to his truck.

"'Free' is always a bargain," she countered.

After the truck rumbled off, Garrett went to work finishing cleaning the stalls. She sat on a stool and watched, not saying a word, but not seeming bored, either. He wondered what Lenny would say to people, because he certainly wasn't about to keep this bit of news to himself. No way.

Garrett was aware of her, of every time she

crossed her legs or stretched or sneezed. Once when she was hunched over a little, her shirt gaped and he could see she was wearing a black bra. He liked red best, but black took a close second. It gave him something to fantasize about, anyway. Did she wear some tiny black thing as underwear?

"You only have the three horses?" she asked after a while, having seen them in the corral.

"At the moment. One's been with me a long while. Apple Annie. These others ended up here over the past week. Haven't located any owners as yet."

"And how many dogs?"

"Six. At the moment."

"Do those numbers change a lot?"

"They come and go. Except for Pete. He stays."

"Abel seems pretty entrenched, as well."

Garrett glanced over at the mutt, who'd made himself at home at Victoria's feet. "He's been hard to place. Not that he isn't a good dog. He's just… attached."

"I haven't seen any cats."

"They keep to themselves. Last I counted, there were three. They do a good job of keeping the rodent population controlled." He spread new straw in the last stall and wondered what would happen next. She didn't seem inclined to leave.

"I brought lunch," she said then, sliding her hands down her thighs nervously.

He didn't know what to make of her—of the adoration in her eyes, her sassiness and straightforwardness. It was an odd and fascinating combination, and he needed to be careful. While he felt an almost blinding physical attraction to her, he would never be good enough for a Fortune, not with his past, not even for a night.

"I pictured you slapping a peanut-butter sandwich together for yourself," she went on when he didn't speak. "Thought maybe you'd like something a little heartier."

He ambled over to where she sat. She straightened as he got closer. Her eyes took on a little wariness. "Victoria—"

"Vicki," she interrupted breathlessly. "Most people call me Vicki."

He let a few seconds pass. "Victoria, I don't need mothering."

"I'm not mothering you. I'm trying to be your friend. Friends do nice things for each other."

"I've got all the friends I need."

"Well, then, you're a rare man. I figure I'll meet lots more people in my life who will become friends. Some just for a little while and some forever. You saved my life, Garrett. That's an unbreakable bond between us."

"Yeah? Well, I'm beginning to regret doing that." He stalked toward the door, not knowing where he was going, just that he needed to get outdoors.

She laughed and followed. "Roast beef sandwich, potato salad and apple pie," she said, a coaxing lilt in her voice.

How'd she know his favorite meal?

"Estelle told me," Victoria said smugly, apparently reading his expression. "Emily and I ate breakfast at her diner this morning. She even packed our lunch in a cooler I'm supposed to bring back when we're done."

He reached the stairs to his front porch, stopped and turned around. "So now Lenny and Estelle both know you're out here visitin' me. You might as well have taken out an ad in the weekly."

"Are you hungry?"

Her cheerful, I-am-never-denied-anything tone made him want to shake his fists at the sky. Instead he shook his head. "I need a shower."

"I'll wait. Thank you," she said seriously.

He bit his lip. She'd gotten her way, and she knew it. "We'll eat here on the porch," he said.

"Afraid if I come inside your house, I'll slip behind the shower curtain with you?" Her eyes took on some shine, not so much in humor this time but provocation, as if daring him.

She had it backward. He was afraid *he'd* invite *her* in. Not only would lunch not get eaten, but maybe dinner and perhaps breakfast, too. He wouldn't mind a good, long time in the sack with her.

"I won't be long," he said, then escaped into his house.

"I'll be right here," Victoria called after him then drew a calming breath. Keeping her hands off him had been torture.

She pulled the cooler from her trunk and set out

lunch on a small, rough-hewn table between two unpadded rocking chairs. She couldn't picture him in a rocker at the end of the day, except maybe if he had an ice-cold beer while watching the sunset for a few minutes. Maybe. She would've said he wasn't a sentimental man, except that the way he treated animals said differently.

She wondered if he really deserved his reputation. He'd been gentlemanly with her—unfortunately. She smiled at that, then she loosened a button on her blouse, sat on a rocker with her knees up and waited patiently for him to join her.

Beyond the way her body felt around him, she liked him. He wasn't like anyone else she knew, sure of himself but not in an arrogant way. The way he touched his animals said a lot, too. He knew how to be tender. She figured he was also very strong. Men who worked ranches and farms generally were. She didn't know anyone else who worked physically for a living.

And he seemed comfortable in his own skin, a very good trait.

The screen door creaked open. Pete stood right away then tracked Garrett to the second rocker, sitting next to his master.

"Is Pete one of your rescued dogs?" she asked.

"We sort of rescued each other. The food looks good." His easy change of subject was marked with a tone indicating it wasn't going to be reopened. He grabbed a wrapped sandwich and dug in.

They didn't talk, and that was amazingly okay

with her. She was a curious person, one who asked lots of questions, wanted to know the how and why of things, but this time she just ate and listened to the land, the wind swirling dirt across the property, horses neighing in the corral, dogs yipping now and then. How different were the night sounds?

After they finished eating, she put the empty containers in the cooler, which he carried to her car.

"Have a safe trip home to Atlanta," he said, blocking her from moving beyond the car.

She forced herself to smile. "I'm not leaving Red Rock yet."

"Your choice, Victoria Scarlett, but don't come out here again." His eyes seemed filled with both desire and regret.

Something roared through her—loss, a sense of abandonment and even more, a feeling her future had just zagged onto another path. "How'd you know my middle name?"

"You're splashed all over the internet, the adored daughter of Atlanta."

"I want you," she said impulsively, probably foolishly but honestly.

"Which is exactly why you need to go now and not come back." Tension coated his words. He fastened the button she'd undone, his fingers grazing her hot skin, making her draw a shaky breath. "You can't be with a man like me, Victoria."

"Why? What's wrong with you?"

"I'm too old for you. I like my quiet life. I don't want bright lights and big cities."

"What makes you think I want more than to sleep with you?" She saw that her words surprised him. Maybe he even saw she was lying. She *did* want to sleep with him, but perhaps he could see more deeply into her and know that she felt something more than that. She shouldn't. It was ridiculous, given their short history. But she wanted more. Her dreams had been full of him. She'd been wanting him for months.

"Princess, you've got a little fantasy going based on me saving your life, and maybe because there's an attraction between us. We won't be acting on it. That's that." He walked straight into his house and shut the door.

Pete had followed him, but Abel let her give him a hug, one she really needed.

Rejected. Emily had been right. Victoria wasn't used to it, and it stung a whole lot. Mattered a whole lot.

"Take good care of him, okay?" she said to the dog. "I think he needs someone to love him."

She had to leave him alone, as he wanted. If she pursued him, pushed him, he would only get angrier, and she'd rather he remember her fondly.

Victoria got into her car, then a half hour later she walked into Estelle's diner, cooler in hand, having lost her good spirits. The noon rush was over, only a few customers sat at the counter, sipping coffee. The redheaded, fiftyish Estelle was leaning her elbows on the counter and gabbing with an older man.

"Everything was wonderful," Victoria said to her. "I'll set this by the kitchen door, Estelle."

"That'd be fine, thanks. Oh, Lenny was here for lunch. Said he met you."

"Yup," Victoria answered, drawing a laugh. She would be as tight-lipped as necessary. Garrett would appreciate her discretion, she was sure. "Garrett was kind enough to show me his rescue operation. He's doing good work."

"Rescue operation? I thought he just took in stray animals."

"He also trains them so that they're ready to be good pets for people." Victoria assumed an all-business mode. She owed it to Garrett to protect him from gossip—and maybe to improve his reputation a little. "That's a nice little enterprise he has going. Well, thanks again, Estelle."

"Sure thing, honey."

Instead of getting in her car, Victoria walked to a park a couple of blocks away. She didn't want to face Wendy and Emily yet, afraid the disappointment of being dismissed by Garrett would be visible on her face. That defeat hurt more than she'd expected and was deepening each minute. She was torn between staying away, as she'd first thought she could, and making a bigger effort to tear down his walls of resistance. Could she accomplish that? Maybe if she had more time…

Caught between the challenge of winning him over and her usual don't-make-waves stance, Victoria sat on a park bench to think. A young mother pushed her toddler in a swing across the way, but otherwise it was a school day and therefore devoid of older, noisier children, giving her the quiet she needed.

He was right about some things—fourteen years was a big difference in age. Wendy had told her he'd moved away a couple of times. What had he done during those exiles? What kind of life experience did he have that she didn't? She was accustomed to the men of her social circle. Similar backgrounds helped smooth the path to an easier getting-to-know-you time in a relationship.

Nothing was similar about her and Garrett, not that she could tell, anyway. She did like bright lights and big cities—it was all she knew. When he'd said he didn't like them, it probably also was experience speaking. She'd only visited Red Rock, so she didn't know about small-town living, especially isolated-ranch living. She didn't think she was cut out for it.

So, what could she do?

She rubbed her face and blew out a breath. She focused on the mother and child playing, heard their laughter, smiled as the little one said, "Higher, Mommy. Higher!"

Emily had asked Victoria about having a family, and she'd answered truthfully. She hadn't given it a lot of thought, except in the way she always had—someday, when she was married and the time was right, it would be the next logical step. But she hadn't hungered for motherhood like Emily.

And Garrett certainly wasn't marriage material.

He'd separated himself from daily life among people for a reason. If she could somehow convince him to sleep with her, that would be the extent of their relationship.

Could she live with that?

No. She knew for a fact she would want more. Much more. He appealed to her on levels she'd never experienced before. He was worth fighting for, but at what cost? Not just to her, but to him. Everyone had the ability to be hurt, even him, no matter how hard he might fight it.

She made the decision then to leave him alone, to relegate him to a bittersweet memory and unfulfilled dream. She would finish her vacation with Wendy and Emily, return to home and work in Atlanta, nightmare-free at last, and move on with her life.

And leave him to live his.

Chapter Four

Garrett was about to bang on Wendy and Marcos Mendoza's door four days later when he spotted the "Baby Sleeping" sign hanging on the knob. It didn't cool his ire but it did temper the force with which he knocked. Victoria Fortune had some explaining to do.

She opened the door. Her shower-wet hair had dampened her yellow blouse. No jeans this time, but slim, dark brown pants. Socks but no shoes. No lipstick.

She looked sexy as all get out.

"Well, Garrett, how nice—"

"What the hell did you do?" With his boots and hat on he towered over her. And while he didn't usually use his height to his advantage, especially with a woman, he was furious enough with this one to make a point.

Victoria stepped outside, pulling the door shut behind her. "Be specific, please."

"You told Estelle I run an animal-rescue operation."

"Don't you?"

"Hell, no. I take in strays now and then and rehabilitate them and find them homes. It's not an *operation*. There's nothing official about it."

"Maybe my terminology wasn't exactly right but—"

"Your *inexact* terminology brought me two horses, eight dogs and five cats in the past two days. And I don't expect the 'donations' to stop. Included in that total are a mother dog and four puppies and a mother cat and four kittens, by the way. That's *fifteen* more mouths to feed. And find homes for. Not to mention spaying and neutering and shots. Plus they need to be isolated until they get their vet check."

"Technically, you only have seven new mouths to feed—assuming the puppies and kittens are being fed by their mothers."

He glowered and she held up a hand. "Just trying to lighten the mood."

"Try a different tack."

"I apologize for what happened. What can I do to help?"

"You can tell Estelle you made a mistake and let her spread the word."

"You could do that yourself."

"You need to eat a little humble pie, princess."

She crossed her arms. "I'm supposed to fly back home in a few hours."

"Then you'd better get crackin'." He spun on his heel and took off, feeling her eyes on him as he strode to his truck. By the time he started the engine, she'd moved to the front of the porch, watching him.

She's leaving....

He'd sort of been waiting for her to show up un-invited again, figuring she didn't like being denied something she wanted, and she'd made no bones about wanting him. He'd been flattered and aroused by it. Dreams of her had become jumbled with re-newed nightmares of the tornado. He wondered if hers had gone away for good.

He took off for home. It wasn't the dogs and cats that would take up his time, except for finding them homes—it was the horses. They took a long time to work with, especially if they'd been injured or abused. These two new arrivals were skittish, not yet letting him check them out, so he didn't know what he was dealing with. But the time involved in caring for them took away from his work, and his work brought him an income. Without money he couldn't continue to support his animals.

For the moment, however, he needed to make boxes to contain the puppies and kittens, a job that shouldn't have been necessary in the first place.

Why had she done it? Did she think he wasn't

good enough as he was, so she wanted to make him seem more charitable, therefore better, to the citizens of Red Rock?

Cursing the tornado that was the source of all his current problems, he pulled up in front of his barn and unloaded supplies. He spent the next couple of hours working in the barn, surrounded by the sounds of puppies yipping and kittens mewling. Strange and familiar dogs milled around, with Pete asserting himself as alpha dog to settle down the new arrivals and establish their place at the ranch.

Garrett had just moved the mamas and babies into their respective stalls when he heard a car approach. The new dogs barked or hid. The rest went to greet the visitor. Garrett didn't recognize the car—or the one that pulled in behind it. Or the next one, which also towed a horse trailer. But as the people emerged, he recognized several from the Red Rock branch of the Fortune family, and a couple of Mendozas, as well.

An hour later, he was still standing outside his barn feeling bewildered when he spotted Victoria's rental car coming up his driveway. She bounded out of the vehicle, her face glowing.

"Well?" she asked.

"I gave away four dogs, one horse and two kittens—when they're ready. What'd you do? Strong-arm your family?"

"Who doesn't want a well-trained pet? They sold themselves. I think more people will show up in the next week, too. Everyone eating at Estelle's got the word, and she'll spread it further. You may run out of animals."

She looked pretty proud of herself—understandably—but she'd also just turned his life upside down. People would be coming to his ranch, interrupting his life. He didn't want that.

"You've got jeans and boots on again. Aren't you leaving?" he asked.

"I changed my flight. I needed to right my wrongs before I left."

He crossed his arms and angled toward her more. "Why'd you do it, Victoria? Why'd you tell people what you did?"

She frowned. "I was trying to help you."

"Help me how?"

"I thought to improve your standing around here."

"Why would that matter to you?"

"Because I know you're a better person than your reputation."

He couldn't remember a time when someone had defended him. Certainly no one had mounted a public relations campaign on his behalf. It made him distinctly uncomfortable.

"May I see the newest members of your menagerie?" she asked.

He figured the puppies were about two weeks old and the kittens only days. The three new adult dogs were all mixed breeds and skinny but gentle. Food and a little attention would turn them into good pets before too long.

Victoria oohed and ahhed over the babies and cooed to the mothers, telling them what good mamas they were. Garrett watched her crouch low to talk to them, her hair curling down her back, her jeans cupping her rear. He wouldn't mind putting his hands there. Wouldn't mind it one bit.

She looked up at him. "How can I help?"

"I'm gonna give the new dogs baths. They all need to be brushed and have burrs cut out. A two-man team works more effectively than one."

She stood and rolled up her sleeves. "Just tell me what to do."

One by one they bathed the dogs, muzzling them first, washing, rinsing, combing, snipping. He treated their ears, checked their skin, then turned them loose, figuring they'd go roll in the dirt. He was right.

Victoria sighed beside him. "That didn't last long."

"They like to smell like the stuff they like."

She was wet and muddy. At some point she'd twisted her hair into a knot at the back of her neck. She didn't seem worried about the way she looked, however, didn't fret about her appearance at all.

"What do you do for a living?" he asked.

"This 'n that," she answered, giving him a sly grin.

He came close to laughing. "Guess I deserved that."

"Guess so, but since I'm not as secretive as you—"

"Private, not secretive. There's a difference."

"The end result's the same," she countered.

He shrugged at her logic, not giving in.

"Anyway," she continued, "I'm the assistant director of sales for JMF Financials."

"JMF being your father's business?"

"Yes. He started it himself when he was twenty-four. We sell and manage financial portfolios, mostly for corporations, specializing in retirement plans."

"So you sell 401(k)s?"

"Sounds exciting, hmm?" She rolled her eyes.

"It could be, if it's what you want to do."

"I don't know what I want to do." She kicked at the dirt, as if measuring how much she should say. "Actually, according to my parents, my primary job is to find a husband, but I haven't cooperated. I did finish college while I was husband hunting, however. My degree is in marketing, but I haven't been invited into that tight circle at work. My family didn't want me floundering after college, so my dad made my brother Shane take me as his assistant director. I think there's resentment from all my brothers because they had to work their way up. I had a pretty good title to start with."

"But?"

"It's a job. I want a career."

"Being a homemaker could be a career."

"I'm not ready for that, much to my parents' disappointment."

Abel bumped her from behind, knocking her legs

out from under her. Garrett caught her by one arm before she landed on the ground. She laughed and wagged her finger at Abel, who barked and jumped around her until she knelt and rubbed him.

She glanced up at Garrett. He didn't release her immediately, but almost pulled her against him.

"I should get going," she said. "Wendy and Marcos are throwing a little party."

He dropped his hold on her. "Special occasion?"

"Oh, someone they want me to meet," she said dismissively.

The way she said it implied it was a man. He tamped down a surge of jealousy, unfamiliar and unwanted. "I thought you were leaving."

"I extended my vacation a while longer." She met his gaze. "I won't be missed at work, and it's been fun hanging out with my cousins."

He walked with her to her car, not knowing what to say. "Goodbye" would've been the best and easiest choice, but he had a feeling he would see her again.

Or maybe not, depending on how her dinner date went tonight.

She opened her door then turned to him, pulling something from her pocket and shoving it at him. "Here. To help with food and shots and stuff."

He glanced at the check, which was folded in half. He had no idea how much she'd written it for, but he figured it was enough to cover his expenses for a while. She thought he was that poor?

"I don't want your money." Insulted, he held it out to her.

"I got you into this mess. At least let me help pay for what I did."

"I don't need it."

She ignored him and got in the car.

"I won't cash it," he said.

"That's your choice."

When she reached for the handle, he held the door tight, then he shoved the check in her shirt pocket. Her breast was firm and full. He pulled his hand out fast, after barely two seconds of contact.

Don't go. Don't go back to Red Rock for a blind date. Don't go back to Atlanta....

He didn't say any of it. She looked at him the way Jenny Kirkpatrick had twenty years ago. He'd had to leave town because of that look—and what Jenny had wanted from him, which he hadn't wanted in return. He'd made a life for himself finally, a life he wasn't willing to risk, not for a fling—because surely that's all it would be—and he'd given up high-maintenance, demanding women.

"Goodbye," he said to Victoria.

"Bye now," she said cheerfully, then shoved the check under his belt so fast he barely felt it, but his imagination dragged out the moment.

He didn't watch her drive off, not giving her that satisfaction, but Abel looked at him as if to say, "You let her *go?*" before he turned tail and walked away. Even Pete seemed disgusted with him.

Curiosity got the best of him, however, and he

opened the check, whistled at the amount, then ripped it up. She probably brought in an above-average salary for someone of her age and experience. He'd bet she got annual bonuses, too, maybe even had a trust fund.

Well, he wasn't running a charity, but doing what made him happy. He could afford the life he'd chosen. He'd been angry at her for what she'd done and had wanted her to feel guilty.

Apparently he'd been too successful at doing that. She'd stayed on in town instead of flying home, would continue to be in the area for however long and she was about to be introduced to someone her family obviously approved of.

It was for the best, he decided, especially as his head filled with memories of Jenny Kirkpatrick.

When he'd been a senior in high school, Jenny had been one of Red Rock's golden girls, a sixteen-year-old, straight-A student with a desire to become a doctor. At eighteen, he was older but really no wiser, not knowing how the world worked then. He just knew she was pretty, and he liked her fine and she liked him, too. Was fascinated by him, in fact. Kind of like Victoria.

Garrett looked out at the horizon now, taking his time to think about Jenny, something he hadn't done in years, knowing it was his meeting Victoria, another golden girl, that was spurring the memories. He needed to analyze the past now, because it could have bearing on his future.

After he and Jenny had met, her grades took a

nosedive, and he'd gotten blamed for it. Her parents forbade him to see her. Her father's wrath had struck fear in Garrett, so he'd done the right thing and told Jenny they were through dating until her parents okayed it.

The never-before-denied pampered daughter had rebelled by running away from home—all the way to San Antonio. Without money, she'd shoplifted food at a convenience store, and the owner had called the police and her parents, getting her the attention she'd wanted.

Somehow that had been all Garrett's fault, too. The Kirkpatricks were the richest people in town, and Jenny the most spoiled girl. Garrett was just... Garrett—poor, fatherless and with a mother who didn't care enough to parent him. He'd finished his senior year then joined the army. Jenny had been sent away to a private school.

Pete barked, pulling Garrett out of his thoughts. Another car was coming up the driveway, towing a trailer, a horse inside it.

Maybe he'd ripped up that check too soon.

Victoria yawned as she carried empty dessert plates into Wendy's kitchen, Emily at her heels.

"What was Wendy thinking?" Victoria whispered. "He's such a bore. And so full of himself." He was a high-tech innovator from San Antonio and let everyone know how successful he was.

"She was thinking he would distract you from your infatuation with Cowboy Freud."

"Seriously?" Victoria looked toward the kitchen door to make sure they weren't being overheard. "And she thought that man out there would do the trick?"

"Okay, I can't put this on Wendy. Your mother set it up."

Victoria plunked her fists on her hips. "I haven't spoken to my mother about Garrett, at least not since the first night when I told her I'd been to see him."

"Your mother talked to our mother, who had talked to Wendy. She hadn't thought anything about Mom's curiosity, just answered questions that apparently your mother gave her to ask. Wendy commented that you seemed taken with Garrett. She didn't know she was being grilled, Vicki, although she is worried about you a little."

"She doesn't need to be." Victoria swiped the dessert plates almost violently with a sponge under running water.

"Really?" Em said, coming up close. "Wendy and I both think you're headed down a dangerous path chasing after him, Vicki. You're bound to be disappointed when he doesn't live up to your expectations."

"You've barely met him and you've decided I'm going to be disappointed?" Fury welled inside her. First, Garrett kept her at arm's length, thinking she was some kind of pampered daughter of society, and now her own family wasn't acknowledging her as a competent adult. "What does Marcos say? He, at least, knows Garrett some."

"You'll have to ask him."

"I will." She dried her hands and returned to the living room.

Her "date" stood. "Wendy and Marcos are putting the baby down," he said.

She sat in a chair next to him. "You never mentioned what company you work for, Derek."

He shifted in his seat. "TexTechtronics."

Ah. "JMF Financials handles your retirement plan."

"Oh, that's right. They do."

Like he didn't know that.

"Would you like to go for a walk?" he asked in an obvious change of subject.

"No, thank you." She couldn't get mad at him for doing her father a favor. He'd been used as much as she had. "I enjoyed meeting you, Derek, but I don't see this going anywhere. I'll be headed back to Atlanta very soon."

He looked relieved. "I see." He offered his hand. "I think I'll head out, then. Please thank Marcos and Wendy again for the meal. It was top-notch."

Marcos had brought it home from Red—delicious, as always. He'd taken a break from work to have dinner and would return before closing later. Friday was a busy night. He'd probably been perturbed at his presence being required.

"Where's Derek?" Wendy asked when she and Marcos emerged. Emily came out from the kitchen at the same time. There was little doubt she'd eavesdropped.

"Vicki sent him on his merry way," Em said. "She got the whole messy plan figured out."

"Oh." Wendy put a hand over her mouth. "I'm sorry, Vicki."

"I'll leave you all to sort this out," Marcos said, giving his wife a kiss.

"A word before you go, please," Victoria said.

He stopped at the front door, looking resigned.

"Should I be afraid of Garrett? Or worried in any way?"

Marcos shrugged. "He lives a quiet life, doesn't cause trouble. It's true he hasn't made friends in the sense that we think of. He doesn't have parties or go to parties. But he's fair in his business dealings, always pays his bills."

"Why does he have a reputation?"

"He's years older than I am. I don't know what happened, except he left town when he was eighteen because of a scandal over a teenage girl. When he came back he picked fights in bars. He left again. Since he came back, he's been a hermit." His shoulders shifted. "He does entertain women, I've heard, but I haven't heard any complaints about his treatment of them. That's all I can tell you."

How often did he entertain? And why did he turn her down? "And you don't know how he supports himself?"

"What am I? The town private investigator?"

Victoria crossed her arms. "You run a restaurant. You must overhear stuff."

"Not anything related to Garrett. He's always seemed okay to me. Look, I've got to get back." He kissed his wife goodbye again and rushed out.

"Why are you so protective of Garrett?" Wendy asked Victoria. "He doesn't even have a job. He likes animals a whole lot more than people."

"Maybe he has good reasons for that. Maybe he was railroaded out of town. Injustice makes me angry."

And because I'm falling for him.

Victoria had to sit and let the idea sink in, without letting her cousins see anything they might report to their mother or hers.

"Are you going to see him again?"

"Yes." That much she knew.

"You have to know a relationship with him would only be short-term," Emily said, looking worried. "And if by some chance it does go beyond that, do you really think you could live his kind of life? Or that he could live yours?"

"No, but I'm also not a starry-eyed teenager. Don't worry. I won't come crying on your shoulder."

Wendy reached out and grabbed Victoria's hand. "You can always cry on my shoulder. I won't say I told you so."

"Me, neither," Em said. "And we won't be talking to our mom about it again, either."

"Thank you," Victoria said with a sigh of relief. "I think maybe I should move to the hotel so you can honestly say you didn't know anything. I feel like I'm crowding you, anyway."

"You're welcome here," Wendy said. "But do what makes you feel comfortable."

"I'll think it over. Thank you." She stood. "I'm going to take a walk. Clear my head."

She grabbed a jacket and headed out. Again it occurred to her that she wouldn't do this at home, not at night, although more from caution than experience. It was quiet here, a car passing by now and then, but no one honked. She could look up and see a starry sky.

Victoria kept walking, ending up at Red. She peeked in the window. Almost every table was full, and in a corner booth was Tanner Redmond, a man whose photo she'd only seen once, when Jordana showed his website to her, but she was positive it was him. He was laughing with a beautiful dark-haired woman who touched his arm now and then as she spoke. When he sipped from his glass, his eyes held her gaze.

She pulled out her cell phone and called her cousin Jordana. "Did I wake you?" Victoria asked.

"It's okay. I always seem to be napping."

"How are you feeling?"

"Better. I'm into my second trimester. It's good. How about you? Are you home?"

"I'm taking an extended vacation in Red Rock—where you should be, I might add."

"Have you seen Tanner?" she asked.

"I'm looking at him right now. He's having

dinner at Red with a very attractive woman who's flirting like crazy with him. Jordana, I'm about ready to go in there and tell him he shouldn't be dating anyone since he's going to be a father."

"You can't do that!"

"Then you get yourself down here and tell him the news. You really can't wait any longer."

"I just need a little more time. But I will. Soon."

"What are you waiting for? You are one of the strongest, smartest women I know. It isn't like you to avoid such a major issue."

"You haven't been pregnant and unmarried, so don't lecture me."

Victoria blew out a breath, calming herself. "You're right. I haven't."

"I'll deal with it in my own way."

"All right."

"And you won't interfere."

Someone tapped Victoria on the shoulder. She spun around. "Marcos! You scared the wits out of me."

"Are you spying on someone?"

She held up a finger. "I have to go, Jordana. Talk to you soon."

Jordana was still sputtering when Victoria ended the call—without promising she wouldn't interfere.

"What's going on?" Marcos asked.

"I was out for a walk, and I decided to call Jordana."

"I heard the tail end of your conversation. Wendy's very worried about her, you know."

"She doesn't have to be."

Marcos gave her a long look. "All right. Um, one thing I thought of after I left the house. Garrett had some trouble out at his ranch a couple of years back. Had to do with a woman, but I don't know more than that. The sheriff was called. But you know small-town gossip. The truth is in there someplace, but you'll have to search it out for yourself at the source."

"I will. Thanks. Oh, Marcos," she said as he turned to leave. "Is that Tanner Redmond at the corner table?"

"Sure is."

"And the woman with him?"

"Don't know. I've never seen her before."

Well, shoot. She was tempted to hang around until they left and check if they were cozy or not as they walked to his car, but that could be hours and she wanted to be up bright and early.

She had a big day planned for tomorrow. It was time to start taking some risks.

Chapter Five

It was Garrett's first breakfast at Estelle's since Victoria had come to town. He'd expected to be the subject of a few raised eyebrows, maybe even a couple of comments. What he hadn't expected was to find Victoria seated at the counter, reading the newspaper and eating pecan waffles and ham, maple syrup coating everything on her plate, as if it was something she did every day.

She didn't look up until the whole place went quiet, then she glanced toward the door, saw him standing just inside it, looked surprised and then waved him over.

He nodded at various customers as he headed toward her, then he took the seat next to her. "You're in my seat," he said.

She looked one way then the other. "I don't see anything indicating that."

"Everyone knows that's my place on Saturday morning." He couldn't tell whether she'd planned the moment or was as innocent as she looked. She wore jeans again and red boots he hadn't seen before. Her blouse was new to him—red-and-white stripes with pearled snaps, like something she'd wear to a hoedown. Not that he'd been to one anytime recently....

"Do you want to trade seats?" she asked.

"Hell, no. Not with everyone watching."

Estelle set a mug of coffee in front of him. "Your usual?" she asked.

"That'd be fine, thanks." He waited until she got out of range, then finished his answer to Victoria. "What I want to know is why Estelle didn't say anything about it to you." He cocked his head. "Or did she?"

Her teeth flashed white in a quick grin. "She might have mentioned it in passing."

"So everyone here has been waiting for my reaction."

"You would know better than I. Seems to me the people around here are overly involved in each other's business, so you're probably right. What's your usual?"

He shifted mental gears. "Two eggs over easy, hash browns, a slab of ham and biscuits and gravy."

She gave him the once-over. "I don't see where you put it."

"I don't eat lunch on Saturdays."

She laughed at that, raising her mug in a toast.

"Did you know I'd be here?" he asked.

"I told you before, cowboy. If you have a particular schedule you stick to, I've never been shown it."

Her phrasing was just vague enough for him to take her answer either way. He decided to let it go, figuring it wouldn't be so bad having breakfast with a pretty woman.

"Want the sports?" she asked, holding up a section she'd put aside.

"Thanks." They sat next to each other, reading and eating, occasionally commenting on something in the paper. Their arms brushed now and then. The first time it happened, she froze for a few seconds. After that, he consciously pressed against her every so often, until she finally did the same. It seemed friendly, almost like an inside joke, but it felt arousing. He couldn't remember a time when such a small, innocent touch had made him wish for a private room, a big bed and all the time in the world.

After a while, Estelle came over. "You two need to kiss, start a fight or take off. No one here's gonna go until something happens. I'm gonna start losing business in a couple of minutes."

They looked around. Customers were lining the walls, waiting for a table, because no one had left. Garrett pulled out some bills and dropped them on the counter. "My treat," he said to Victoria.

"Why, thank you." She had a bit of maple syrup

stuck in the corner of her mouth. Licking it off wasn't an option, so he gestured to her.

"What are your plans for the day?" she asked, dipping her napkin in her water and wiping her mouth.

"Errands, then back to see how many new residents have arrived."

She looked contrite for a second or two.

They walked out together, him nodding occasionally, her waving and calling out goodbye. He'd lived quietly in Red Rock for years. He didn't want life to change, yet she was already changing it.

"How did last night's dinner go?" he asked as they neared her car.

"Somehow my mom and dad managed to set me up on a blind date. I love my parents, but they've been pushing too hard to get me married. It's driving me crazy."

"Did you like the guy?" *Say no.* If she liked him and ended up staying in town because of the man, Garrett would have to see her now and then. It wasn't an option.

"No, but he didn't go for me, either, so it ended just fine. Do you have a girlfriend?"

The question caught him off guard. He answered without thinking. "No."

"Good," she said, getting into her car. "See you around."

Good? He didn't want to get caught staring at her as she drove off—especially since everyone in the diner seemed stuck to the window, watching, holding their collective breaths—so he went to his truck without hesitating, putting an end to the crowd's anticipation.

Good? he thought again. She should've figured out by now that he wasn't a man who wanted ties, not even a girlfriend, much less a wife. Maybe he hadn't been clear enough. He'd just have to flat out tell her.

He'd do that next time there was an opportunity so there wouldn't be any confusion about the issue.

When he pulled up to the hardware store, he saw her car outside. This time he was more than a little suspicious. He couldn't imagine a single reason for her to be shopping at a hardware store, but there she was, studying a rack of picture hangers.

"Well, hey," she said, looking surprised, an expression she'd perfected. "Fancy meeting you here."

"Come here often, do you, princess?"

"Wendy just framed a bunch of pictures of the baby. I volunteered to pick up hangers. What do you think? Which ones are the easiest to use?"

He grabbed a package and passed it to her.

"Thanks. What are you getting?"

"This 'n that."

She laughed, then she tapped his chest with the packet. "See ya."

When she was shining it on for someone, she was irresistible. Ray Cleft, who owned the hardware store, got swept up by Victoria's charm to the point where he was blushing. Garrett shook his head, but he also moved to a place in the store where he could watch her get into her car. She had the audacity to smile knowingly and wave, then off she went.

By the time he reached the feed store, he was no longer surprised that her car was parked there. He was a creature of habit—Estelle's, hardware store, pet food, then groceries, every Saturday, like clockwork. Despite what she'd said, someone must've told her.

"Marcos and Wendy get a new pet I haven't heard about?" he asked as she stood contemplating doggy chew toys. "I've been trying to sell Marcos on a dog for a long time. He always says no."

"Hmm? Oh. Yes, you're right about Marcos. I'm getting these for your dogs. You know, so they can chew away their frustrations. And look at these adorable bandanas they can wear. I think I'll get a dozen. The dogs will look even more adoptable when they look cute, too."

Garrett didn't try to talk her out of it, figuring there was no purpose in trying to change her mind. No one said no to her.

He was surprised twenty minutes later when he pulled into the grocery store parking lot and didn't see her car. He even admitted to himself he might be a bit disappointed. But when he came out of the store later there she was, standing next to his truck when he pushed his cart up to it.

"I didn't want you to think I was stalking you," she said, a twinkle in her eye.

He raised his brows.

She laughed. "I know. 'And yet, you're here, princess.' That's what you're really thinking, right?"

"Close enough. What do you want, Victoria?"

"To come out to Pete's Retreat and help with the animals."

He started loading his groceries into the truck bed. "It's up to you."

Her big brown eyes widened comically. "Stop the presses! Garrett Stone didn't tell me no!"

He didn't give her the benefit of even a tolerant look. "You should probably change your fancy clothes first."

"Already in my trunk. Be prepared, you know? I'll follow you." She turned away.

He cupped her arm, made her face him again. "I'm not ever gettin' married, Victoria. Nor am I lookin' for a girlfriend."

An expression crossed her face that he couldn't interpret, then she said, "You know, Garrett, I never would've thought I'd get such a kick out of getting muddy in somebody's barn, either. I'm keeping myself open to new experiences, cowboy. Maybe you should try that yourself sometime. Change can be good."

She was lecturing him? She'd just finished college, had been cloistered all her life, and she was telling *him* how to live?

Regretting he hadn't discouraged her from coming to the ranch, he drove home, his temper simmering. She was right behind him.

Seven dogs greeted them—Pete, Abel, the three

dogs who'd come a couple of days ago and two who'd been waiting in the yard that morning when he got up. He was down to three horses again, one more having been taken yesterday.

"Goodness!" Victoria said as the dogs surrounded her. "You've added more. Where do they come from?" she asked, all innocence.

"I'm sure you'll be pleased to know that word of my *rescue operation* has spread as far as San Antonio."

"As well it should. A lot of people are having to give up their pets because of the housing downturn. Instead of leaving them behind, people are thrilled to find a no-kill site like this. I know I would be." She gave Abel his rubdown as he rolled his eyes in rapture. "Won't the word that you aren't running a shelter spread, too?"

"Probably. It's just being ignored because it's convenient to some people's way of thinking." He grabbed the two grocery sacks with perishables then walked over to her. "Did you get my message earlier? I want to be sure you understand me, princess. I may be set in my ways, but I also know myself well. I've been to hell and back a couple of times and lived to tell about it. Having a woman around for more than a night doesn't sit well with me."

"What happened to you?"

"I try not to look back." He headed toward the house, he could hear her following after a few seconds.

"If you lived to tell about it, why not tell me?" she asked when they reached the door.

He'd set down his grocery sacks to unlock the door. When he glanced back at her, he could barely see her face, hidden behind two bags as she was. Just her eyes. Her beautiful chocolate-diamond eyes.

"It's an expression, you know? I don't talk about it."

"But you just did. So feel free to continue."

He ignored her, leading the way into his house, wondering what she thought of it. He'd seen pictures on the internet of her parents' mansion when it'd been on a holiday home tour for some charitable organization. He could just about fit his place into their living room.

He liked his place a hell of a lot better.

In the kitchen they unpacked the groceries in silence. He couldn't tell if she was mad or hurt. They seemed to have had long periods of silence between them, mostly comfortable. This one had an edge to it.

"I'll get my clothes and change," she said.

"Bathroom's across the living room and down the hall."

After she left, he leaned his hands against his countertop for a minute and blew out a long breath. He'd had women in his kitchen before—women always seemed to want to cook for him, as if showing off their wife potential—but he'd never felt as if anyone belonged, not until Victoria moved around the space with him. Maybe because she hadn't been gabbing the whole time. Maybe because she seemed to know where things belonged without asking.

Maybe because he kept having images of her in his bed, naked and willing...

From the bathroom, Victoria heard the front door shut. Not slam, exactly, but shut more loudly than necessary. What was he so ticked off about? He hadn't seemed to mind her popping up everywhere he went this morning. She'd been testing the waters with him, seeing what she could get away with, and he'd seemed, well, not unhappy, anyway.

One thing she'd learned—when his emotions were involved, he dropped his *g*'s. *I'm not ever gettin' married, Victoria. Nor am I lookin' for a girlfriend,* he'd said. She liked knowing that about him, figured it would come in handy sometimes.

She carried her clothes to the living room and hung them over a chair. His house was about what she'd expected—old, durable furnishings, but the rooms were spotless, a masculine decor with lots of wood, devoid of accessories or art except for one oil painting of his ranch. She got close enough to look at the signature—Liz. Was she one he'd spent a single night with?

Jealousy reared its ugly green head, so she joined him in the barn. Abel had been waiting at the door much like Pete did for Garrett. Abel bounced around her, as if making sure her attention would be on him and not the new dogs or the plethora of puppies and kittens.

She took a deep breath as she walked across the yard, enjoying the open air. Yes, it smelled like dust and animal, but it was a clean scent to her. And the near silence of the place healed something in her she hadn't known needed healing. Usually her head was full of words and images, things she needed to do for work or at home or with friends or family. She rarely had a moment to think, just think.

Victoria found Garrett talking to one of the horses. She was about to tease him about being a horse whisperer when the horse nuzzled him. Victoria sat on a nearby bale, Abel at her feet, and watched Garrett halter the horse and lead him out to the corral. She waited until they were inside the corral before joining them at the fence. Garrett walked him, talking the whole time, his voice soothing.

"Do you ride?" he asked Victoria as he passed by.

"Some."

The next time around, "Do you enjoy it?"

"Mostly."

He gave her a look at her short answers and kept walking.

Next pass by he said, "Ever taken a fall?"

"Twice."

He shook his head, but he smiled, as if he couldn't help it. "Break any bones?" he asked as he approached again.

"My left arm. Now I can tell when it's going

to rain hours before it starts. I also scattered my brains, according to my brothers."

"Ever get 'em back straight?" he asked.

"Depends on who you talk to."

He laughed then. Victoria draped herself over the top railing. She loved watching him walk, loved watching him encourage the horse. He'd be a wonderful father…

The thought blared in her head. *He'd be a wonderful father?* Where had that come from? Since when was that issue of any interest to her whatsoever?

Shaken, Victoria dropped to the ground and headed into the barn. She crouched outside of the puppy pen and played with the puppies, who were awake and crawling all over each other, making yipping sounds. Mama had climbed out of the box for a rest but hadn't gone far. She got a drink of water then seemed to be debating whether to return to her pups or enjoy her freedom a little more. She compromised by coming up beside Victoria but not jumping back into the box.

"Are you worn out, Mama? I can't imagine taking care of one, much less four. And where's the father, hmm? You're here doing all the work, and he's out howling at the moon somewhere."

Garrett would never do that, she thought. He'd be there, come hell or high water. He would protect and support and never turn his back on his responsibilities. Everything about him told her, but especially the way he handled his animals, the permanent ones as well as the strays.

The fact he liked animals better than people was a big loss to humanity. She could picture him cradling an infant in his big, tender hands. She could almost feel him holding her through the night, keeping her safe, making her feel loved.

"You okay?" The man himself crouched down beside her, startling her.

"Yes, why?"

"I called your name five times."

"I'm sorry." She looked at him with different eyes now. He would make a wonderful husband, a loving father, a tender, exciting lover. She'd fallen hard for him, and there was nothing she could do about it. She cupped his cheek, moved closer to him, waited for him to pull back. But he didn't, so she kissed him, a long sigh of a kiss, so exquisite her throat burned.

"I admire you more than anyone I've ever met," she said. "You are so responsible and kind. You have some give to you, but you won't compromise your principles."

He couldn't hide his discomfort at her compliment fast enough. She saw the starkness of surprise and appreciation—and then maybe disbelief. Had no one ever complimented him before? Openly appreciated him?

"That's experience, Victoria. The times I've compromised, I've regretted it."

He stood. She followed suit. "Do you have siblings?" she asked.

"Nope." He headed to another stall.

"What about your parents?"

"Couldn't have been born without 'em."

She laughed. "A few more details, please."

"My father was mostly absentee. He was in and out of my life for a few years, then he disappeared. I've never gone lookin' for him. My mom lives in San Antonio, but I don't see her much. She's a nurse at a doctor's office. I have been a disappointment to her all my life, and an embarrassment most of my life."

He'd recited the words matter-of-factly—except that he'd dropped the *g* when talking about his father. "I heard you left town a couple of times. Where'd you go?"

He talked to the second horse just as he had the first, ignoring her question until the horse calmed. "I went in the army the first time. Second time I worked on an oil rig in the gulf."

"Were you running away?"

"You could say that."

"From what?"

"The first time because I'd been accused of something I didn't do but didn't have the resources to correct. Small towns have long memories, so when I came back, I found no forgiveness, no acceptance. I got into a lot of trouble, bar fights, speeding tickets, you name it. I couldn't find work of any measure, so I left again." He grabbed a rake and worked the dirt floor, his movements taut and quick. "When I came back I had matured. I didn't need to fight anymore. And I'd saved enough money to buy this property. Pete showed up the first night and refused to leave, even though I tried my damnedest to get him to go. Satisfied?" he asked, giving her a look.

"Maybe sometime you'll fill in the gaps, but, yes. It answered questions." She followed as he guided the second horse to the corral and worked with him.

"How about you going first," he said. "I'll bet your childhood doesn't resemble mine much."

"I was doted on all my life," she said, unembarrassed by her upbringing, although sad for him. "After having four sons, my parents were thrilled to have a daughter. I wasn't denied much. I went to finishing school, took piano and ballet lessons, attended a private university, and joined the Junior League as soon as I was old enough."

He got out of hearing range, so she stopped talking.

"I'll bet the whole city of Atlanta knows who you are," he said as he approached again.

"My photo shows up in the newspaper society pages a few times a year, mainly for charitable works. I didn't do anything to earn my status except to be born to James and Clara Fortune, but I hope I've been a good steward of the name."

He circled the corral again. She enjoyed every second of being able to watch him openly. He looked at her with the same intensity, the same desire. It thrilled her, agitated her, excited her.

"Sounds like a good life," he said, coming close again.

"Yes, it has been, and maybe I've been frivolous but I've also volunteered many, many hours for worthy causes, just not jobs where I had to get dirty. But, honestly, Garrett, nothing has made me feel as good as working with you and your animals." She reconsidered her words. "I know I've only helped bathe the dogs, but I'd like to do a lot more, if you'll let me."

He kept walking after her last statement. She couldn't see his reaction, couldn't see if it mattered to him, although he was usually good at hiding how he felt, anyway. At the beginning, she'd thought he didn't care about anything but himself and his own small world, but she was beginning to think he cared too much, and this was how he dealt with it.

"You know, Garrett," she said as he approached again. "You don't have to be what people expect you to be."

"Meaning what?"

"When you came back the last time, people expected you to be the same bad boy as when you left. You've lived a quiet life, not giving anyone fuel anymore, but not really proving you've changed."

He kept walking. She waited what seemed like hours for him to near her again.

"You expected me to be a princess," she said. "Do you still think I am?"

"I don't think you're used to anyone having a bad opinion of you," he answered. "I think it would bother you a whole lot if anyone said something bad about you. Like if my reputation tainted yours, for example."

She considered that as he made another loop with the horse. His expression was questioning when he made the turn toward her. "Are you saying it doesn't bother you if someone says something bad about you?" she asked.

"You're answering with a question now, are you? Very sneaky." He kept walking.

"I do what I find works."

Victoria was having the time of her life. She liked everything about him—except maybe how reclusive he was, which was a big negative. And how resistant he was to anything long-term with a woman, which was a bigger negative.

"This may shock you, but I don't fall into a swoon over such things," he said, coming near again, his eyes sparkling.

She laughed at the image. "I probably would," she said, being honest. "I don't have particularly thick skin."

"What a surprise. Have you ever gone against your parents' wishes?"

She thought about that until he got close again. "Not in a big way. The usual teenage rebellions, but minor ones."

They spent the rest of the day doing chores, most of them having to do with keeping things clean for the animals. She stalled going home for as long as possible, but finally there was no work left, at least for today. Tomorrow it would all start again. Garrett's routine was just that—routine. Except for the changes because of what she'd done, all the additional animals.

Before she left, they sat in his rocking chairs on the porch drinking sweet tea. She was getting hungry, having not eaten since breakfast.

"May I come tomorrow?" she asked.

He hesitated a few beats. "Aren't you leaving town?"

"I haven't booked a return flight."

"Why not?"

"I wasn't ready to." Wasn't ready to give up on him, anyway. She wanted to curl up in his lap, but she knew if she tried he would not only reject her but tell her not to come back. She planned to ask for another week off, giving herself time to let him get more used to her. They'd come a long way today with the revelations they'd shared with each other.

"It's been a while since I had a real vacation," she said.

"You call this a vacation?"

She smiled. "If you think of it as a change of scenery and change of pace, yes, this has been one. Plus my nightmares have gone on vacation here, and I'm not ready to test them back home yet. So, may I come back tomorrow?"

When he didn't answer, she said, "I've got your back, Garrett."

He gave her a sharp look. "Meaning?"

"Meaning whatever we say or do here, stays here. This relationship is precious to me. If rumors start around town, it won't be because of anything I've said or done."

"I don't need a champion, Victoria."

Yes, he did, but she wouldn't defend him again. His hurts were buried deep. She didn't want him to relive them. "You've made that clear. I won't try to boost your reputation for the general population again. Actions speak louder than words, anyway. I'll prove that to you. So, knowing that, may I return and help?"

He nodded, not looking at her.

It was enough for now.

Chapter Six

"I already talked to Shane, Dad," Victoria said on the phone the next morning. She was lounging in a chair on Wendy's sunporch, waiting to leave for the ranch. "He's fine with me being gone another week. I haven't had a real vacation since I started working for JMF."

"I don't have a problem with you taking more vacation, Victoria. I just want to know why. Why there? Why now?"

"I'm having a good time with my cousins and the new baby." Which was the truth, although she hadn't paid all that much attention to the baby. Victoria had never babysat; her brothers hadn't married and had children yet, either. She wasn't used to being with an infant so tiny.

"Here's your mother," her father said abruptly.

"Hey, sugar. What's this about staying on an extra week? Does it have to do with a man?"

"No, ma'am."

"How was your dinner the other night with that friend of Marcos?" Her tone was perfect, just the right amount of curiosity and innocence.

"Let's just say it wasn't a match."

"Oh? Why not?"

"How can anyone define such a thing? No sparks, on either side."

"Have you seen that…cowboy again?"

"It's a small town." She couldn't wait to get out to the ranch again.

"I've been thinking I might like to join you girls for a few days. I'm sure Virginia wouldn't mind seeing her new granddaughter again."

Victoria saw through the ruse. "It's a full house, Mom."

"You and I could stay at the hotel. Let Wendy and Em have their mother to themselves."

Victoria had always found it interesting that the two Fortune brothers didn't get along but their wives did, even to the point of socializing quite a bit. However, Victoria absolutely did not want her mother to fly in, with Aunt Virginia or alone. Victoria had no doubt at all that her mother would somehow ruin what was growing with Garrett. But if Victoria fought it…

Maybe a little reverse psychology? "That would

be fun, Mom. I'm sure we can figure out *something* to do here that would interest you."

A few seconds of silence ensued. "I just remembered. This week I've got the hospital guild luncheon. I'm co-chair this year, you know."

"What a shame." Relief rushed through Victoria. She'd dodged a bullet.

"Sugar, you know your father and I want what's best for you, don't you?"

"Of course I do."

"Every girl falls for a man once in her life who isn't exactly right for her."

"Your point, Mom?"

"I know you well. Your silence about that cowboy is saying more than you think."

"Even if I were interested, he's not. Does that set your mind at ease?"

"Why, yes, it does, sugar. Very much so. You stay in touch now, you hear? You've been too quiet all week."

Like most of her girlfriends, Victoria checked in with her mother at least once a day. Her current lack of communication had probably been the trigger for her mother suspecting something was going on with Garrett. She would try to phone more often.

"Oh, there you are," Wendy said, breezing into the room carrying the baby, who was bundled in a knit blanket. "Marcos just left for Red, and Em's blow-drying her hair. Can you watch Mary-Anne for a few minutes? I want to grab a shower myself. Thanks." She put the baby in Victoria's arms and left.

The seven-week-old infant usually slept a lot—or cried a lot. But her eyes were open now and she was peaceful. Her mouth was puckered, her hands closed into tiny fists tucked under her chin. She smelled... pink.

After a few minutes Emily joined them. Mary-Anne had drifted to sleep. "Want me to take her?" Em asked.

"We're fine, thanks. You can take her when she's colicky." Victoria snuggled the baby closer. "How goes the Baby Plan?"

"Adoption's starting to seem more and more unlikely. They want couples, at least the private agencies I've contacted. They can afford to be choosy. I think I'm going to make an appointment at a fertility clinic. If they can't find a match for me, I don't know what I'll do."

"Maybe your list of requirements is too exact."

"I'm entitled to that." She moved to stand at the window, looking out at the garden.

"I still don't see why the rush, Em. You're only thirty."

"If I meet a man, go through the courtship process, plan a wedding and *then* get pregnant, I'll be thirty-two at the very least—and I want several children. I want to be a young mom, with energy. I've been looking for a man, you know that. No one's ever been the one."

Victoria thought that no real man could ever

measure up to the ideal that Emily had created in her mind. Even a sperm donor probably couldn't. She was setting herself up for disappointment in a big way.

"I don't know how you aren't craving one of your own," Emily said, coming close.

Victoria was starting to understand maternal need a little, but she figured it had more to do with a certain man. A man who made her want to have children with him.

Wendy joined them before Victoria could answer. She handed over the baby. "I don't know when I'll be back," she said, hugging her cousins.

"Call if you're going to be gone overnight," Em said with a wink.

A girl can dream. "Cell coverage is spotty out there, you know."

"That and 'My battery was dead' must rank one and two in the most-clichéd-excuses book," Wendy said, her mouth twitching.

"I'm a big girl."

"You're on the Pill, right?" Em asked.

"Yes, Mom." She hadn't really considered they would sleep together today until Emily and Wendy made it seem like a real possibility.

It all depended on what the man in question wanted. Or *allowed.* She was pretty sure he wanted. Everything about the way he looked at her said so.

The drive to the ranch sped by, then she had to wait while a pickup truck drove toward her up Garrett's driveway. She didn't recognize the driver as she waved back to him. She also couldn't see a dog crate, either empty or full.

"You're my fourth visitor today," Garrett said as she climbed out of her car, trying to calm a joyful Abel at the same time.

"Down," she said. He jumped up. "Why does he listen to you and not me?"

"Abel," he said. The dog looked at him. Garrett made a quick motion with his hand and the dog sat.

"That's all it took?"

"He'll stay there until I release him. Like this." He made a different gesture. Abel popped up. "He's a smart dog. He picked up commands in a couple of lessons."

She bent to scratch his ears. "Who were the other visitors?"

"First one wanted the remaining two kittens once they're weaned. Second one was looking for her own dog who'd disappeared. Didn't find him here, but if hers doesn't come back, she'll take one of the new dogs. She'll wait until he's gone through training. The last one was from a San Antonio television station."

"I'll bet that went over well."

He tossed his head. "Right. I got my shotgun out."

"You didn't!"

"You're so gullible." He grinned at her then headed for the barn. "'Course I didn't. I just threatened to get it."

"Because you're nobody's headline."

"You got it. So, how was your morning?"

"Nice. Wendy made us some amazing French toast with strawberries."

"Do you cook?"

"I get by. Nothing fancy, but I enjoy it."

"What's your specialty?"

"Pasta with whatever vegetables I have on hand."

He opened a stall. "I put all the horses in the corral. If you're game to clean stalls, I wouldn't mind the help."

"Sure. Let me greet the rest of the animals first."

Soon she grabbed a mucking fork and got to work. Because he mucked twice a day, it took him about fifteen minutes for each stall, which meant he finished two to her one. She sang along with the country music playing from a boom box he kept nearby. He cocked his head at her a couple of times when she sang dramatically loud and off-key, but they didn't talk.

"How often does an owner find their lost dog here?" she asked when they were done.

"It's happened a couple of times. In both cases, the dogs wore tags, so it was only a matter of making a call."

"Do you crate them?"

"I've never had to contain a dog except to quarantine when necessary. Once they pass the vet test and are released, they seem to like it here. Never had any get into big fights, either. Pete puts a stop to 'em right away."

"Are you always successful in finding homes for the strays?"

"I can be persuasive when I want to be."

She smiled at that. "I don't doubt that a bit. Plus you don't let them go until they're trained. That's a bonus for most people." She rubbed her arm. "It's been a while since I've done physical labor."

"Or it's gonna rain."

"That's it! That's what it feels like. How'd you know?"

"It's in the air, a couple hours out."

"So, what else needs to be done before the rain hits?"

Victoria had spent a lot of time being a team player—in high school, college, on charity committees and at her job. She was a self-starter, but was usually okay with being part of a collegial group. Working side by side with Garrett felt productive and satisfying. He led, she copied. She tried to anticipate what he needed from her as they got the horses back into their stalls, cleaned out the puppies' and kittens' pens and put out fresh food and water for the rest of the pets.

"Rain's about here," he said as they left the barn.

She sniffed the air, acknowledging the distinctive scent. "Maybe I should just head home before it hits."

"Your choice. I was just going to offer you lunch. Although I guess we worked through lunch. An early dinner? I've still got a couple of portions from Red."

"That would be great, thanks."

She was surprised to find fresh vegetables in his refrigerator and made a green salad while he heated enchiladas, rice and beans. They sat at his small dining table in the kitchen nook and looked out the window into his back acreage, filled with brush starting to green out for spring, and tumbleweeds. It was stark but not ugly.

He offered her sweet tea. It was a perfect meal. Once again they didn't talk much as they ate, and it was okay with her. Comfortable. The rain started, noisy and cocooning. She didn't mind it a bit.

She leaned back when she was done, pressing her hands against her stomach. "I'm stuffed."

"No dessert?"

Her interest perked. "What kind?"

"What would make you feel not too stuffed?"

"Pie."

"What kind?"

"Pie."

"Well, then, you're in luck." He set their plates in the sink. "Blackberry pie. Want coffee?"

"No, thanks. And just a sliver." She wondered where he'd gotten it. The pie plate looked like it came from someone's kitchen, not store-bought.

"Ice cream? Whipped cream?" he asked before he brought her the plate.

A few fantasies came to mind at the image of whipped cream. "Just plain, thanks."

The first jolt of thunder hit when she took her last

bite, followed by a crack of lightning. Then the rain started pelting down, loud and hard.

He jumped up. "Thunderstorm. Hadn't expected that. I need to make sure everyone's inside and shut the barn doors."

"I'll help."

He eyed her briefly but thoroughly. "It won't take me long. No sense both of us getting drenched." He grabbed a rain jacket then rushed outdoors.

Victoria followed, deciding to watch from the porch. She'd never seen a Texas storm—except the tornado, of course. When she pushed open the screen, it hit Garrett in the back.

"What's wrong?" she shouted, as thunder rumbled.

He turned around holding a puppy in his arms. "It was on the rocking chair, along with this note. It's wet. I can't read all of it. Just take it inside for now."

She gathered up the frightened, shaking puppy, who looked a little older than the ones in the barn. She glanced at the note then. "Wait! Garrett, wait a second. It looks like the note says, 'I can't keep the pair of them. Their mama died.' There's another puppy."

Garrett cursed a blue streak the likes of which Victoria hadn't ever heard. It fascinated her, all those words strung together like that. "You go tend to the rest," she called out. "I'll put this one in the house and hunt for the other."

"No, I'll do it."

"I won't melt in the rain, cowboy. Just go."

He hesitated, then he said, "There's a flashlight on the kitchen counter and a jacket by the front door. Look around the perimeter of the house first, through the lattice. It couldn't have gone far, and it probably wouldn't venture into the open."

By the time she was armed with flashlight and jacket, the rain had intensified to sheets. Thunder cracked and pealed. Lightning flashed in the distance, but was inching closer. She shined the flashlight at the foundation, behind the shrubs that lined the front of the house. If a puppy cried out at all, she couldn't hear it above the pounding rain. Rain soaked her jacket, weighing her down and running into her boots, filling them and making it hard to lift her feet.

Still she kept looking, panicking a little more each second, hoping she wouldn't be too late. She'd noticed yesterday that Garrett had been digging along the perimeter of his house, as if he was going to plant more shrubbery. It wouldn't take too deep a hole to trap a puppy. If it filled with rain…

She was on her hands and knees calling, "Here puppy, puppy, puppy" for the hundredth time when Garrett dropped to his knees beside her.

"Go inside," he shouted. "I'll take over."

She shook her head. She had to find this puppy. She had to. It had become critical to her. "I've checked both sides of the front. You take the right side. I'll go left."

He didn't argue but scrambled up and away. In

time they met at the back of the house. The thunder and lightning had moved on, their noise in the distance now. The rain continued, although not as hard or loud. She heard a sound that froze her in place. Then she heard it again, coming from nearby.

"Garrett!" she yelled. "Over here."

He slid on the mud, ending up next to her as she shined her flashlight toward the sound, under the raised foundation. Fortunately the lattice only covered the front and sides of the house, but it left the back open for the puppy to tuck himself farther under. Now he was mired in mud, trying to dig his way out, his cries breaking Victoria's heart.

"Move," Garrett said, shoving her, trying to dig an escape route for the dog but only creating more mud. He shifted his body parallel to the house, but the puppy remained out of reach.

Victoria ripped off her jacket and copied him from the other side. "I'm smaller," she said. "I can get under there."

"Stop! You could get trapped in the mud," he yelled.

She didn't say anything. She inched her way closer, then suddenly felt Garrett's hands on her legs, his fingers wrapped around her calves, holding her tight. "Come here, baby. Come on," she urged the puppy. His eyes shined back when she spotlighted him, but he didn't, or couldn't, move.

"Push me closer," she shouted to Garrett, keeping a hand out. Her clothes sucked mud as he pushed her a few inches, until she could grab the pup by the scruff of its neck and drag him to her. "Got him! Pull me out!"

Out she came, mud coating her. She didn't care one bit. She shook some of the muck off her shirt then wrapped the dog in it.

Garret put his arm around her and guided her to the back door, which led into the laundry room. Her mud-filled boots were hard to walk in, weighing a couple of pounds more than usual. Once they were inside, he told her to stay put, moved past her then quickly returned with towels. He yanked off his jacket and pulled his shirt over his head. Then he took the puppy from her, wrapped him up and held him close to his chest.

"Drop your clothes in the set tub, then you can go shower. I'll rinse everything before I dump it all in the washer." He turned his back to her, giving her privacy.

Getting the boots off was the hardest. It was like her feet were stuck in cement. Huge sucking sounds accompanied her efforts, then she was free. She dragged her clothes off and tossed them into the open tub, added her bra and panties, then wound a towel around her body.

She started to pass by Garrett.

"Are you okay?" he asked.

"I'm exhilarated. My adrenaline is sky-high. We saved him, Garrett. We saved him." She rubbed noses with the puppy then pulled Garrett down for a kiss, mud and all.

"I'll put some clothes inside the bathroom door

for you," he said, touching foreheads, a surprising depth of emotion in his voice. "If you dig around in the cabinets, you'll find a blow-dryer, I think."

"Thanks." She hurried down the hall, anxious for a warm shower, even more anxious to get back to Garrett and the puppies.

She'd just climbed into the shower when she heard the door open. "Here you go," he said.

Want to join me? The words stayed trapped in her throat. "Thanks," she said instead.

She didn't linger to dry her hair, knowing he needed to shower, too. She put on the shirt he'd left, a soft flannel plaid, and rolled up the sleeves. His sweatpants were way too big around and long, and his shirt covered her almost to her knees, so she just wore that. The fact she was naked underneath made her feel vulnerable but also excited.

Victoria found Garrett in the kitchen, still shirtless, gently bathing the puppy while its littermate romped across the floor and back. An old-fashioned towel rack held her bra and panties.

"I figured you wouldn't want them in the wash with your jeans and all that dirt," he said, trying to contain the wriggling puppy who probably hadn't seen a bath before. He eyed her lingerie. "Pretty in pink, princess?"

"I own every color of the rainbow, cowboy. What's your favorite?"

"Red."

"Predictable. Black is probably second."

"You've got me figured out, I guess."

"Just going with the odds." She felt her nipples hardening at his interest, was aware of straightening her spine some, arching her back a little at the direction of the conversation. "I'll bet you sleep in the buff."

"You'd win. You? Tell me you don't wear some old sorority house T-shirt, or former boyfriend's football jersey."

"I've never quite managed being comfortable sleeping naked. What if there's an emergency in the night and there's no time to get dressed?"

"How many times have you had an emergency in the night?"

She felt her cheeks heat. "Never."

All he did was smile.

"Do you really think it feels different?" she asked.

"I can't speak for anyone else." He settled the puppy in a clean towel. "You did good out there, Victoria. Better than I could've. Here." He put the bundle in her arms. "I need a shower."

She watched him go, thought she heard him say "A cold shower," but wasn't sure. She sat at the kitchen table and dried the ball of fluff, then set him—her?—on the floor with its sibling. They pranced around, their tiny nails clicking against the wood.

Thirsty, she poured two glasses of iced tea and carried them into the living room, keeping an eye on the puppies until Garrett returned.

When he did, he was wearing a T-shirt and

sweatpants, for the first time not looking like a cowboy, but comfortable…and ready for action.

Victoria was ready, too.

Chapter Seven

The cold shower didn't work. Garrett took one look at Victoria seated on the couch with her legs tucked under her and knew he was a goner. She was naked under his shirt, her breasts moving whenever she did. Plus she was brave and caring—and not nearly the princess he'd originally assumed she would be.

Because she kept her gaze locked on his, he avoided the couch and headed to the kitchen. "The pups are probably starving."

"Do you think they're weaned?" she asked after a slight pause.

"I doubt it, or else the person who dropped them off wouldn't have brought them here. I figure they're about four weeks, given their behavior. I've got some bottles and formula. I'll have to get some puppy food tomorrow. Would need some soon anyway for the other pups."

"May I feed one?" She'd followed him into the kitchen. The pups bounded in, too, whimpering.

"Sure."

He'd had to feed pups and kittens before, so he had a stock of appropriate bottles and formula. Soon they were settled on the floor with towels and cushions, the puppies sprawled on their bellies, drinking noisily. Victoria never stopped smiling, especially when her pup wriggled closer, its tail wagging. After they'd emptied their bottles, they both fell asleep. Garrett made a bed in a cardboard box for them, one they couldn't escape. They didn't even open their eyes when he set them inside.

"Would your other mama dog nurse them, do you think?" Victoria asked, taking a seat on the sofa again and picking up her glass. "She's only got four puppies, after all, and room for more."

He sat in a chair across from her and took a long drink himself. "I thought about trying, but she's a small dog. She couldn't produce enough milk right away. These two can be weaned soon probably. Plus, they need to be checked by the vet before I introduce them to any of the others."

"Did you take the new dogs to the vet?"

"He comes here. It's easier. Yeah, he checked them out early this morning. By the way, the one you rescued is a boy. The other's a girl. Want to name them?"

"Dee and Dum," she said right away. "Dum's the boy, of course, for getting himself stuck like that."

"I'd say he was adventurous and not content with the status quo."

She laughed. "Of course you would. Do you name all the animals that land here?"

"The dogs for sure, so they'll respond to commands by name. It's part of their training." He looked at his mantel clock, surprised it was only eight-thirty. He'd thought it was at least ten. It was still raining hard, although the thunder and lightning had moved on. "Guess I'm not going to make it to Red to pick up my meals," he said. "I checked the phone lines a while ago. Nothing."

"I checked my cell. No signal. Won't they guess that the storm kept you from coming?"

He nodded. Now, what to do about Victoria? "I don't want you out there trying to drive home," he said finally. "Flash floods can happen in an instant, and it's already muddy and wet."

"That's okay with me. I want to help feed the puppies during the night."

"I don't expect they need to eat during the night anymore. How will your family react to your not coming home?"

"They'll figure it out. I'll check my phone for service now and then, but they'll know what happened."

"I don't have a guest room. Only my bedroom and an office."

She patted the couch. "Here's just fine. I'm easy."

She smiled then, her eyes darker than usual and heavy-lidded—which could be arousal or exhaustion.

"Easy?" He doubted it. "Complicated, I think."

"Good. I like that you think that."

He stretched out his legs, crossed his ankles. "I appreciated your help." Especially since he didn't usually accept help from anyone. Of course, she hadn't let him reject her offer, either.

"I got you into this mess," she said.

"Yes, you did."

She grinned. Her hair wasn't dry yet, and it had begun to curl, a lot. She wasn't wearing makeup. Her toenails were painted a deep purplish color. She looked even younger than twenty-four. It was a stark reminder of just one of their differences.

He went to the front door. "I need to do a final check on the animals. Make sure everyone weathered the worst of the storm okay. There's a blanket chest in my bedroom. You'll find bedding and pillows."

Garrett shrugged into his still-damp rain jacket then a dry pair of boots. Pete came out of his doghouse at the end of the porch to walk to the barn with him. Abel greeted them and tagged along as Garrett made the rounds of the stalls and boxes. The new dogs were still wary, but they seemed to be getting along all right. The two new horses tossed their heads at his approach. He took a little time to talk to each of them, calming them.

The storm had probably upset them, as well as

being in new surroundings. They would adjust soon. The mother dog and her puppies were snuggled together in a heap, Mama giving Garrett an I'm-so-tired look before tucking her head among her babies again. Mama cat gave him a similar look. They should all do well until morning, he decided. The light of day would bring new questions and problems, but also answers and solutions.

He and Pete returned to the house. Garrett had given up years ago trying to convince Pete to come indoors. Even during cold and rainy nights he liked his doghouse, always seemed to want to stand guard.

Garrett gave him a thorough rubdown before returning to the biggest question and problem, the one on his sofa. He hoped she'd gone to sleep.

He had a feeling she hadn't. Even if she was bone-tired, it wasn't late enough for bed.

The couch was empty. He glanced in the kitchen. Not there. He couldn't hear a sound of movement anywhere. He hoped she hadn't taken it upon herself to climb into his bed.

He hoped she had....

Garrett found her in his bedroom, bent over his blanket chest and pulling out linens, his shirt riding up her slender thighs. He found it hard to believe she hadn't heard him come inside. He leaned a shoulder against the doorjamb and admired her.

Her arms full, she turned around. "Oh! I didn't know you were back. That was fast."

"They didn't require any work, just a once-over."

"I'll get out of your way." She started to pass him. He didn't budge. "Except that you're in my way."

It'd been a long while since he'd spent intimate time with a woman, and this one was more than willing. How long was he supposed to resist her eagerness? She was a modern woman who'd already pointed out that she was only interested in sleeping with him, so what was holding him back? It was exactly the kind of relationship he liked.

In bed, none of their differences would matter, not their ages or social statuses, not their upbringing or life experience. She would head back to Atlanta, their curiosities satisfied, the tension gone. She could return to her ivory tower, and he to his animals and—hopefully—peace and quiet.

"Garrett? What's going on?"

He cupped her face. "Would you share my bed tonight?"

"Why?"

Her question so caught him off guard that his mind went blank.

"Because I'm here and convenient?" she asked. "Because we just saved a puppy's life and we're high on adrenaline from the experience?"

"I think the answer's more basic than that," he said finally. "You said you wanted me."

"That was yesterday."

What had he done to lose his appeal to her in a day? He didn't know how to respond to that. He backed away, giving her space to get past him.

"Now I know you better," she said, not budging. "And like you even more. I'm attracted to the whole man now. That could complicate things. For me, anyway."

She was right about that. It could be a big complication. "Well, girl, that's a decision only you can make. I'm drawn to you for you, not because you're standing here bein' willing. If that's enough, okay. If not, I'll see you in the morning."

"First of all, I'm a woman, not a girl, so don't call me that again. Second, this is all getting too unromantic to me. It's losing its passion and spontaneity."

"If everyone took the time to think things through, we'd have fewer problems in the world— and fewer surprise babies."

Victoria didn't want to lose the spark, didn't want this to become some kind of business deal. She wanted to get carried away, to get lost in his arms, but she didn't want to leave with regrets, either.

Won't you regret more giving up the opportunity to make love to him?

Yes. A great big yes.

He took her by the shoulders and turned her toward the hallway before she could tell him yes. "Good night, Victoria."

Angry at herself for blowing the opportunity, she marched down the hall into the living room. She didn't bother making the couch into a bed, just tossed a pillow down then yanked a blanket over her.

She heard a puppy whimper for a few seconds then stop. *I know just how you feel,* she thought. She squeezed her eyes shut. Her day had been long and tiring. Sleep should come easily. Instead, she lay there imagining what she was missing, hoping he was having trouble getting to sleep, too. She tossed herself onto her side, punched her pillow. He was probably sawing logs already. Naked.

Men.

Victoria rolled onto her stomach and groaned into the pillow. Suddenly she felt hands on her back, large, competent hands.

"Relax," he said, bending close to her ear.

"What are you doing?"

"What I should've done earlier."

He was romancing her, she realized. Caressing her.

She did relax. His hands felt wonderful on her back. He had strong fingers that massaged out kinks she hadn't known she had. He found every one of them. He didn't push her shirt up, but worked through the fabric, even over her rear. The blanket slid down and off her legs, then his hands were touching her skin at last as he worked his way down to her feet. His thumbs pressed into her instep, making her groan with pleasure.

He slid his palms up her legs again, this time pushing up her shirt over her rear, which he kneaded and stroked. He dragged his tongue over her, bit lightly into her flesh, as he slipped his hand between her legs and caressed with featherlight touches. Fire raced through her body, fast and liquid. Sounds came from her mouth that she'd never heard before. She'd known he would be gentle. She hadn't guessed how sexy gentleness was.

He rolled her over, put his mouth on the hot, aching core of her. *Backward,* she thought. *We're doing this backward. We shouldn't have started this way.* She needed his mouth on hers first. And yet…

She'd never felt like this before, the center of complete attention, complete adoration. His tongue did exquisite things to her, making her rise to meet him then making her wait, almost there, then cold air washing over her for a few seconds, then his warm mouth again. She shook uncontrollably, grabbed his hair, arched her back. He rose up before she could climax. She wanted to curse and praise him at the same time.

His mouth finally came down on hers, his tongue meeting hers, dueling, demanding and yet not making her feel dominated. His chest was bare. She ran her hands over his flesh, felt the ridges of muscle and bone. He sat up and slowly, so very slowly, unbuttoned her shirt, spreading it open, cupping her breasts, running his thumbs over her aching nipples.

"You're perfect," he said just before he sucked a nipple into his mouth, his teeth dragging along the hard flesh. He pulled her onto his lap, her legs straddling him, then he carried her down the hall to his bedroom, his big hands cupping her rear. By the time he set her on the bed and pulled the shirt off her, she felt light-headed but the rest of her body felt full and heavy. She'd wanted passion and romance. She was getting it.

He didn't wait for her to help him take off his sweatpants, but he shoved them down and off, grabbed protection from his bedside table, then joined her in bed, stretching out beside her. He fanned out her hair, ran his fingers through the curls, dragged them over her breasts.

"How can you hold back like this?" she asked. Every nerve was aflame with need.

"When something's important, you do it right." He looked into her eyes.

"You're making a memory."

"Damn straight."

Why? she wondered. Why did it matter to him that she take a memory with her? She laid a hand on his chest and memorized him, too. He wasn't bulky like a weightlifter but he was strong and muscular, his way of living enough to keep him fit. She had to use the gym in her building.

Finally he put a hand over hers, stopping her exploration, pressing it against his chest. Then he kissed her, tenderly, thoroughly, passionately, moving over her without stopping the kiss, sliding into her slowly, filling her then pausing. His body went rigid, he made a low, guttural sound as he pulled out then thrust in. It was all it took for both of them. The mutual explosion was loud and fast and long…and excruciatingly beautiful. She felt connected in every sense of the word, heart, soul and body. A memory, indeed, framed in her mind forever.

She hoped he felt the same.

He gathered her close and rolled with her, settling her on top of him, wrapping her up, both of them struggling to breathe, to settle, to relax. She wanted to cry, so she burrowed her face against his neck and squeezed her eyes shut, staving off tears of magnificent fulfillment. She wanted to stay in his arms forever.

After a while he pulled up the covers but didn't let her go. She wanted him to say something. She wanted to know he felt the same things she did.

Eventually he climbed out of bed for a few minutes. When he returned, they lay on their sides looking at each other. He pulled her leg over his, then draped his arm over her hip, splaying his fingers over her rear, the tips teasing her, making delicate circles, keeping her level of desire high.

"Nothing to say?" he asked.

"I'm pretty sure you could tell I enjoyed myself." She ran a finger across his mouth. "Would this have happened if I hadn't been stuck here?"

"Yes." His gaze held hers. He didn't even blink until she broke the contact herself.

It was exactly what she'd wanted to hear.

"Think you can sleep as you are, or do you want a T-shirt or something?" he asked.

She smiled leisurely. "I'll let you know if I start feeling uncomfortable."

"Are you sleepy?"

The sound of rain on the roof lulled her, as did the steady feel of his heart pumping against her hand. She could easily fall asleep, but she didn't want to give up a moment in bed with him. "Sleep isn't what I'm craving at the moment."

"Craving? Hmm. That's a good word." He moved his hand over her breast, cupping her, running his thumb over her nipple. "There's a lot more to you, it would seem."

"I don't flaunt." Which wasn't entirely true. She'd unhooked an extra button with him more than once. She let her hand drift down his body, finding him ready and willing. "I could say the same for you."

Garrett sucked in a breath and savored her exploring touch. He shoved her hair aside, pressed his lips to her neck, tasted the perfume that was Victoria, distinctive and tempting. As their bodies warmed, he threw back the covers, sat with his back against the headboard and straddled her in his lap. He barely felt her weight, yet she was settled heat to heat on him. He lifted her, guiding her onto himself, letting her take him inside then go perfectly still.

"We fit," she said breathlessly.

Too well, he thought. *Far too well.* Even knowing the consequences, he accepted what she offered and gave back in full. They merged and melded, found pleasure and satisfaction. Her mouth was hot on his, demanding yet yielding. Giving and receiving. Powerful beyond measure. Twice would not be enough. One night would never be enough.

She arched back, squeezed him tight, let out a

long, low sound that reverberated through him until he couldn't resist and climbed atop the same peak of pleasure. She collapsed against him, breathing hard.

It struck him then what he'd done—or, rather, hadn't. "I didn't use protection," he said, panic twisting inside him. However well they fit together physically, it was all they could have.

"I'm on the Pill."

"I don't take chances. Ever."

"It'll be fine, Garrett. Really."

He had to believe her, had to hope there weren't any consequences for his carelessness. And for a long time he stayed awake, holding her and wondering just what kind of hole he'd dug for himself.

Chapter Eight

Garrett was gone when Victoria woke up in the morning. They'd made love somewhere around five-thirty, then he'd tucked the blankets around her and got out of bed. "Go back to sleep," he'd said.

She had. For hours.

Victoria stretched, pulled his shirt on and went in search of him, not finding him in the house. The puppies jumped and whimpered at her, making her laugh, then she poured herself a cup of coffee and took it with her to the shower. Maybe he'd be back by the time she was done.

Her cell phone rang as she passed through the living room. She picked up the phone, saw it was her mother calling and noticed there were seven messages awaiting her, as well. All from her?

"Good morning, Mom."

"Finally. Victoria, I have been scared out of my mind. I was about ready to book a flight. Where have you been?"

"I'm right here in Red Rock. We had a big storm and it wiped out phone service." Victoria picked up a magazine from the coffee table, *Saddle and Rider.* Then she noticed her fingernails. Not only was her polish chipped, she'd split two nails.

"Well, I worry. Mothers do that."

"If something happened to me, don't you think Wendy or Emily would let you know? Unless you hear otherwise, assume I'm fine, okay?"

"You don't have to get snippy about it. I thought the vacation was doing you some good, but you're still uptight."

Victoria closed her eyes for a moment. Her mother was right. She was being defensive because she knew she was doing something her parents wouldn't approve of. It had made her secretive, and she was usually open, especially with her mother. "I apologize, Mom."

"I'll be glad when you're home again and I can see for myself how you're doing."

"Despite apparent evidence to the contrary, I really do feel good."

They ended the call on a happier note, then Victoria showered and went in search of Garrett.

Everything was quiet. His truck was in the yard, the horses in the corral, but no dogs were out and she couldn't hear music or him talking to the animals.

She almost tiptoed to the barn door, then heard the sound of metal hitting metal, but light taps not hammering. Abel spotted her and woofed, then others followed suit, including Pete. Garrett came out from behind a wood divider wall she'd never paid attention to before. He looked guilty…or something. Definitely uncomfortable. Was he regretting making love with her?

"Good morning," she said, not moving toward him.

"Sleep well?" He stuffed his hands in his pockets, something she'd never seen him do.

"Never better." What was going on? He was the most self-confident man she knew. He couldn't have any doubts about whether she'd enjoyed herself last night, so why did he look so hesitant? "You were up early."

"My internal alarm clock never changes. The braid suits you."

Her hair always kept falling in her face—and sometimes into muck. It seemed sensible to get it out of the way. "It's practical."

"You need a hat, then you'd be set. The Cowgirl Princess."

She gave up waiting for him to make a move. She hugged him. His arms came around her, loosely at first then all enveloping. "Are you hungry?" he asked after tipping her head back for a lingering kiss.

"For food or you?" she asked.

"Given the number of surprise visitors I have these days, I would say food. I waited to have breakfast until you woke up."

"How about I fix breakfast and you go back to whatever it was you were doing. Give me about twenty minutes."

"Sounds good."

"What *were* you working on?"

"Um, just doin' a little work on a saddle."

The *um* threw her off. When he chose to speak, he spoke well, without hesitation. It was almost as remarkable as the dropped *g.* "May I see?"

He made her wait a good thirty seconds. Finally he said, "What happens at the ranch, stays at the ranch, right?"

"Of course, Garrett."

He took her by the hand into a room largely hidden from the barn section and reached only by a small doorway ingeniously blocked by another fake wall. She hadn't thought about how much wider the barn seemed from outside than inside. Now it made sense.

And what a room it was. Organized chaos, she decided. There were saddles on racks, long tables with tack laid out, shelves full of boxes and tools, lots of tools, few of which she could put names to.

"What is this?" she asked, wandering around.

"It's how I make my living. Custom saddles and tack. A few other items."

"You make saddles?"

"I embellish them. These are for show and parade horses. I also repair museum pieces. That's what I was picking up at the airport that day. A museum in Montana had sent some old leather pieces they'd received." He rested his hand on a saddle next to a worktable. "I've been working on this one all morning. The horse and rider will be in the Rose Parade this year. Actually, I'll be doing four saddles and other paraphernalia for her group."

The work was detailed and exquisite. He did leather tooling, but also set gems in silver, intricate work, especially for a man with such large hands and long fingers. "Remember that bolo tie you wore at the airport? Did you make that?"

"One of my first pieces. Most show people want jewelry to match their saddles, so I learned how. I do belts, too."

"You're an artist." She picked up a necklace of hammered silver and orange jade. A saddle with matching silver and jade was perched nearby. "This is stunning, Garrett. I hope you're charging what this is worth."

He shrugged. "It pays the bills and keeps the animals fed."

"How does word get out about you?"

"Through satisfied customers."

"You've never advertised?"

"Wouldn't know where to start."

"How much time do you put into it?"

To give himself something to do, Garrett straightened a few tools. "A couple hours a day." He could sense the wheels turning in her head, the business-woman coming to life. To distract her, he tugged on her braid. "Breakfast?"

She left reluctantly, looking over her shoulder. Now that his secret was out, he could go back to work hammering silver for a belt. It was an original design, his own take on the Navajo conchos but with a Texas touch, more a look of mesquite, intricately carved.

He worked with all kinds of gems, precious and semiprecious, his well-hidden safe containing a treasure trove of stones, including some chocolate diamonds a client had sent to be made into earrings and a necklace. They were the diamonds he likened to Victoria's eyes, especially when they'd glittered as he'd made love to her.

Garrett worked until she showed up with a plate in each hand piled with country-fried potatoes, scrambled eggs, bacon and toast.

"I would've come to the house," he said, making space on a counter.

"I didn't see a dinner bell," she said. "And I figured it'd stay warmer if I just brought it."

"Plus you want to use this setting to push some kind of plan you hatched while you were cooking."

Her cheeks turned pink. "That's how my mind works. My degree is in marketing."

"I remember. These are great," he said after sampling the potatoes, which had just the right amount of crisp. Personally, he would've left the skins on, but he wasn't complaining.

"I could create a global network for you on the web," she said earnestly. "You could command top dollar."

He aimed his fork at her. "You know, princess, I may live in the middle of nowhere, and I never did set foot in a classroom after high school graduation, but I figured out what the market would bear. I negotiate now and then, but I've always been willing to walk away from a job. It's all been on my terms. I have no interest in changing that."

"I get that, Garrett, I do. Most artists just want to be left alone to ply their craft. That's where I would come in. You wouldn't have to do a thing except produce the final product."

"Nope. But thank you for your interest." He said it in way that meant the discussion was over.

"You haven't even heard my ideas."

He hadn't seen her this animated before and didn't want to dampen that excitement. Nor did he want to mislead her.

"Okay, here's the deal," he said after giving it some thought. "You put together a solid, workable business plan and we'll talk about it." That ought to keep her busy—and happy—for a few days. She threw her arms around him and thanked him again and again, so he figured he was doing the right thing, at least for her.

"What are your plans for the day?" she asked as they finished their meals.

"I need to fix a better box for the new pups."

"Oh! Do they need to be fed? I didn't even think about it."

"I fed them. They're good to go awhile longer. It'll give me time to get to town and pick up my meals at Red. They'll be wondering."

"They're closed on Monday, but I have an in with the manager, you know. I'm sure Marcos would meet you at the restaurant if you give him a time." She looked away for a second. "Or I could pick up the food when I go to town."

"I wouldn't want to trouble you."

"I need to change clothes. And get my laptop." She met his gaze, a challenge in hers.

"Why?" he asked.

"So that I can work here. It would be much more efficient if I could put together the plan with you available on the spot for questions. Plus I could help you with the animals so that you could spend more time in your shop."

"Are you talking about staying overnight?" Although the idea of her being here with him all day, every day, excited him, her staying went against his personal rules, rules that had worked fine in the past.

But she didn't answer, putting the burden on him to say which way it would go.

"It's not a good idea," he said finally, picking up his silver mallet and starting to work again so he wouldn't have to see the disappointment in her eyes. "What would people say, Victoria?"

"Does it matter?"

"It does. It should matter to you, too."

"I haven't been mingling with people much, mostly just my family. Who would know except them? It's not as if I have a reputation to maintain here."

"But I do."

"Oh! Of course you do. I'm so sorry, Garrett. Truly. I was only thinking of myself. It was just so good last night."

Damn good. Excellent. Satisfying in ways he had never been satisfied. Still, he couldn't give in to the temptation of her spending every night in his arms. He wasn't sure he could give her up.

"Okay," she said. "Let me do this much. I'll go to town and pick up your meals. Only Marcos will know about that. And I can stop by the feed store and get the puppy food you need. I can take the pups to the vet, too. Anything else you can think of?"

He was probably making a big mistake, but he said, "Go ahead and bring your laptop and work here, at least during the day. As long as no one sees your car too early in the morning, it should be fine."

She kissed his cheek. "My parents would love you."

He doubted that. "Why?"

"You're a gentleman. They would appreciate that."

"You don't normally hang around with gentlemen?"

She cocked her head, as if considering that. "Not like you. You're old-school."

"I slept with you out of wedlock. And it wasn't the first time I've done that," he said, giving her a look.

Her eyes widened. "You weren't a virgin? I'm shocked, cowboy. Shocked."

He lifted her onto the workbench. She opened her legs, letting him get close. "You shocked me a little last night."

"How?" She went all flirty on him, fluttering her lashes, her lips curving in a totally sexy way.

That you matched me so well, in every respect. "I'll take the Fifth on that."

"Chicken." She grinned. "I enjoyed you, too. You have excellent moves."

He hadn't felt as if he'd been using moves, but just reacting and responding. As she'd said last night, they fit.

She wrapped her legs around him as he kissed her. He'd enjoyed this morning beyond any in his memory. It was nice to wake up to a beautiful woman by his side, exciting to be kissing her in his workshop, where no other human had been. And way too easy to get used to.

"I'll clean up the kitchen then take off," she said, finger combing his hair. "Call me on my cell if you think of anything else I can pick up."

"I will, thanks."

He lifted her off the workbench then followed her to the big barn door.

"Sure I can't interest you in a quick roll in the hay?" she asked.

Before he answered, the dogs started barking. A vehicle was coming up the driveway. "It's your fault we can't," he said, taking the empty plates from her and setting them aside.

"Guess I can't clean up the kitchen, either. Too bad."

He laughed. They went into the yard as a county sheriff's car pulled up.

"Garrett," the man said, hitching up his pants. He left his hat in his car, which Garrett decided was a good thing. Not an official visit.

They shook hands. "Cletus. How's it going?"

"Can't complain." He looked at Victoria expectantly.

"This is Victoria Fortune," Garrett said. "Victoria, meet Deputy Cletus Bodine. He was my arresting officer a few times in my wild youth."

"The days of the bar fights?" Victoria asked, shaking the deputy's hand.

"He grew up. Been walkin' the straight and narrow for a long time. Except…"

Now what? Garrett thought, figuring Victoria had to be somehow responsible for whatever came next.

"It's come to my attention that you're running an animal shelter. You gotta have a license for that, you know?"

Garrett gave Victoria an I'll-handle-this look before she could pipe up. "I'm doing the same as I've always done, Cletus. Strays just end up here. A misunderstanding arose about this over the past week, but it was just that, a little communications snafu. I've been trying to let people know it isn't true. Meanwhile, more animals have landed here than usual, but I've also found more homes."

"Mind if I look around?"

Although it was phrased as a request, he wasn't really asking. Garrett knew he didn't have to comply, but felt he should, proving he had nothing to hide. "Don't mind at all." To Victoria he said, "Thanks for taking the pups to the vet." He figured she'd slip into the house for her purse and the dogs as soon as he and Cletus went inside the barn.

She held out a hand to Cletus. "Nice to meet you, Deputy."

"Same here, miss."

Garrett had forgotten the empty breakfast plates sitting just inside the barn until he spotted them. He saw Cletus take a look, too.

"A Fortune gal, Garrett? Really?"

Garrett said nothing. He knew the ridiculousness of it without being reminded by someone else. Pete came protectively to Garrett's side, as if sensing something was amiss. Abel sat and watched, attentive. The other dogs were unusually quiet as well, picking up on the tension.

The sound of Victoria's car leaving relaxed Garrett. He told Cletus what had happened to set off the influx of animals.

"I don't think I've been out here since you called to have Crystal evicted. That woman sure did want to stay."

"Not a high point of my life," Garrett said.

"We're all entitled to one crazy woman, I suppose. Me? I had more'n you." The deputy chuckled, gave him a slap on the back and took off.

Crystal had been the straw that broke Garrett's back when it came to women. He'd only intended to spend one night with her, but he'd enjoyed her and let her stay two more nights.

Then he couldn't get her to leave—and then she'd revealed her true colors. She'd pulled everything out of his kitchen cabinets, broken what could be broken, destroyed his home, as well as his fleeting affection for her gender. He'd thought she was different. He'd been right. She was worse.

He'd had to call the sheriff to tame her. The embarrassment of it still haunted him, so he'd put his old rules back into place and had held steady to him. No girlfriend. No wife. Lesson learned.

Or so he thought. He was involved with another woman who wasn't right for him, although in an entirely different way. He couldn't picture Victoria destroying his house, but he hadn't thought so of Crystal in the beginning, either.

Frustrated, he took the empty plates into the kitchen. As he washed the dishes, including the many pans she'd used, he considered Victoria's suggestion for his business. Did he want to expand? Maybe not become a shelter, but a sanctuary? There were good ones around the country, but there was room for more. And if his designs could bring in enough money, he wouldn't constantly have to be fundraising, which was one of the biggest headaches of such endeavors.

Realistically, could he do that?

Not without a plan. And not without help. He also couldn't see himself spending an entire day working on saddles and jewelry. He liked being with his animals too much for that. But if he hired someone to clean the stalls and crates, maybe do the feeding, then he could work with the animals, playing and training. It would depend on what kind of animals he took in. There were circus animals always in need of homes, and Hollywood actor animals. Did he want to take in anything exotic? Elephants? Tigers?

He didn't think so. He was a basic man.

Basic, as in he didn't mind dirt or living without an electric dishwasher or a swimming pool. He liked his air conditioner, though, and the internet and satellite TV for all those long, quiet nights.

Basic, as in he enjoyed hearty, filling food. And sex.

Victoria's face came to mind, not at all a basic woman. He'd spotted her checking out her fingernails while she'd been eating breakfast, recalled how perfect they'd been when they'd walked through the terminal that first day. He'd bet a month's income her nails had never looked like that before.

Her mind fascinated him. She was bright and competent. And game, he thought, for just about anything. He never would've pegged her as adventurous.

No, not basic at all, but multifaceted and complex. How long until she tired of her foray into ranch living and its isolation? This extra week of vacation? Less than that?

Those were the biggest questions of all.

Chapter Nine

When Victoria returned to the ranch, she planted herself in Garrett's workshop with her laptop and got to work. She would need to confer with a CPA and probably a tax attorney, but first she needed a general plan. A plan Garrett would agree to, where he wouldn't have to be concerned with involving himself in the day-to-day operations. He only wanted to create. She understood that. And he wanted time with his animals. He wouldn't be Garrett without that. She would figure out a way.

He'd brought Dee and Dum into the shop, giving them playtime away from the other dogs.

The sounds of Garrett's tools were almost rhythmic. His presence alone soothed her. Every once in a while she found the chance to just stare at him and enjoy the sight. Every so often, she could feel his gaze on her, as well.

After a few hours, he said, "Cletus noticed the breakfast plates," as he polished a silver piece.

"Is that a problem?"

"I don't expect he'll spread the word, but I wanted you to know, in case you run into him again."

"Okay." She saved her work, stretched and rolled her neck. She'd had enough for one day. "Do you want me to bring in the horses?"

He stopped what he was doing, stared at the counter for a second or two then looked at her. "I'm done for the day. If you'd like to bring the two new horses in, that'd be great. Apple Annie could use a ride. We usually spend some time on the property every afternoon. Thanks."

"You're welcome. I'll put the pups and my laptop inside the house first."

She was aware of him saddling the mare as she brought one of the other horses into his stall, then he grinned at her, looking like a kid as he took off at a canter. He'd been right—he couldn't spend all day working at his trade. He needed movement, action and freedom. She needed to build that into his plan.

She wondered how he would feel about having help.

Hired help or…her? She was more excited by working on this than any project she'd been given at JMF Financials. It may have a lot to do with the man, of course, but beyond her attraction to him was the challenge the work presented. She could finally use her education, apply it to a real-life situation, even though she didn't really know what she was doing.

But she did know what he needed.

Garrett didn't come back for an hour, then didn't come inside for another half hour, probably grooming Apple Annie. Victoria fixed a salad, slipped a tray of Carne à la Mexicana, a Red specialty, into the oven and then set the table. She'd even bought napkins to replace the paper towels he normally used. His face was windburned but relaxed as he leaned against the kitchen doorjamb.

"Dinner'll be ready in about five minutes," she said. She could smell horse on him, not a bad smell but a strong one.

"No time for a shower first?"

"Go ahead. Everything will keep that long."

"Thanks."

She was tempted to join him. The only thing that stopped her was the possibility that someone might drive up and interrupt them. Since her car was out front, one of them needed to be able to answer the door.

When he joined her in the kitchen he didn't give her a kiss or hug or even a pat on the rear. He walked past her, opened the refrigerator and pulled out a beer, holding it up to her.

"Yes, thanks," she said, so he grabbed a second, opened it and set it next to her plate.

"How far did you ride?" she asked after several minutes of their usual silence.

He looked startled for a second, as if he'd forgotten she was there.

Which totally annoyed her.

"Out to the river, then along it for a while. Everything's greening up." He dug into dinner again. He didn't gaze longingly at her or reach for her hand or indicate in any way that he wanted her to stay.

Even after dinner while they were doing dishes, he didn't touch her. Finally she folded the dish towel over the oven handle and plunked her fists on her hips. "So, one night was enough for you?"

"Pardon me?"

"You slept with me once and the need is gone?"

He stiffened. "Did I say that?"

"You haven't kissed me since breakfast." She craved him.

"What is it you want?" he asked, crossing his arms.

"To make love with you again." Really, was he that dense? "Wasn't last night good enough?"

"Last night it stormed. We didn't have to worry about anyone driving up and seeing your car."

"Which doesn't answer my question."

"Hell, yes, it was good. Unless you were in a coma, you already know that."

"So, it's only worry about getting caught that's stopping you now?"

He leaned toward her. "Victoria, if I lay a hand

on you right now, I won't stop. I can't take that chance."

It was all she needed to know. She grabbed her purse and headed outside. He followed and watched as she got into her car. She didn't head for the driveway, however, but the back of his barn, where her car would be well hidden unless someone paced the entire property.

She came back up to him and waited expectantly for his reaction.

His eyes glittered as he scooped her into his arms and carried her into his bedroom, dropped her on the bed, then landed on top of her. "You're a problem solver."

"When I have a need."

He dragged his lips along her jaw. "A need. That's a good word." He kissed her then, finally, with heat and demand and a need of his own. "What do you think your cousins would say if you stayed here with me?"

She pulled back a little. Had she heard him correctly? "You want me to?"

"When you got in your car I realized how much I didn't want you to leave. If your car stays where it is…"

"My cousins had mixed reactions."

He rolled onto his side, although he kept his body close and his hand on her arm. "Had?"

"I packed all my clothes and brought them with me." She pressed her fingers to his mouth. "I was hopeful. Let's not overcomplicate things. It's a week, cowboy. Six days, actually. That's all."

"After that we do business via phone and email between Atlanta and here?" he asked.

"If you decide my plan will work for you."

"How will you handle your parents?"

"I'll call a lot. Do you lead off every round of lovemaking with unromantic conversation?" she asked, a little exasperated. "Do I need to go out to the living room and have you come get me again?"

He smiled, a slow, sexy smile, then worked the snaps of her shirt and pushed the fabric aside. "Red," he said, sliding a hand over her lacy bra. "Thank you."

"I aim to please."

He laughed then. She didn't know why nor did she care. She only knew she would get to spend the rest of her vacation with him—and that he appreciated the things she did for him.

She reached for his buttons. He grabbed her hand and eyed it. "You got a manicure."

"And a few pairs of gloves."

"Like I said, a problem solver. So, what are you gonna do about this problem I seem to have developed in the past little while?"

"I thought you'd never ask." Time marched by. She had no idea how many minutes passed, but at some point she was able to say, "Problem solved?"

He pulled her up and planted a kiss on her mouth.

"Damn, you're good." Then he rolled her flat on her back and said, "But I'm better."

And then he proved it.

Days passed. Spring took hold; the countryside came alive with bluebonnets, red-orange Texas paintbrush and yellow gorse. Victoria's vacation was coming to an end, but her business plan wasn't ready yet.

Maybe she'd stalled a little, spending more time with the animals than on the computer. Dragging her heels wasn't usual for her, but she'd mastered it in the past week. If Garrett noticed, he didn't say anything. He spent a lot of time working with the adult dogs, getting them trained so that he could find them homes. Two new dogs had joined them. Garrett was running out of room in a hurry.

Victoria had made two trips into San Antonio to speak to financial experts, but the trips had resulted in producing even more questions. Maybe she was in over her head. She didn't doubt her marketing abilities. What she doubted was coming up with an estimate of costs for him, both start-up and ongoing. He needed to know exactly what he would be getting into. That was critical to her.

It was Saturday afternoon. They'd gone to town to run errands, but not together. She'd visited her family, catching up, surprised to find Emily still living at Wendy's.

And now Victoria and Garrett were in his workshop, working independently. She watched him don magnifying glasses so that he could insert small stones into earrings. He'd finished a saddle with matching stones earlier in the week. The client would be picking up the items on Monday. Victoria wanted to be there to see her reaction.

Actually, she wanted to be there to see every client's reaction to every item he worked on. She'd fallen totally, completely, forever and always in love with him. How that could happen in two weeks was a mystery, but she knew it with all her heart. He was everything she hadn't known she was looking for.

"I'm going to tell my parents I'm staying on another week," she said, testing the waters with him. Since she could only see the back of his head, she couldn't tell what his reaction was—except that his shoulders jerked a little.

"Why?"

"I haven't completed the plan, and there are aspects of it that I can't take care of in Georgia. I need to be in Texas." Which was sort of the truth. It would be easier being able to talk to her sources in person rather than through some form of technology, but it wasn't absolutely necessary.

"Your parents weren't happy when you took a second week. What do you think they'll say to a third?"

"My father could fire me, I suppose, but I've decided that wouldn't be a bad thing."

He set his tools aside and spun his stool to face her. "In what way?"

"I haven't been happy there, at least not with the

work. I've enjoyed hanging with my family more, but selling 401(k) plans isn't what I went to college for. Plus maybe the lesson I've learned these past couple of weeks is that working for and with my family is too easy. I haven't stretched. No one has asked me to or expected it of me. I've been stagnating."

"Stagnating? Really?"

"Now that I've seen a different side of the working life, I can identify what I've been feeling. You're happy with your work. It's obvious in everything you say and do. I want to be happy with my work, too." She shut down her computer and closed the lid.

"Do you plan to stay with me?" he asked.

"That would be my preference." It felt as if they were making a business deal, no emotions involved in their decisions. "Would you mind? Things have worked out okay here, haven't they? We haven't argued. I cook. I clean up after myself."

"You do pretty up the place. I've never had place mats before. Or flowers on the table."

Or a willing woman in your bed every night, all night. "See? I do have value."

"I never denied that." He came up to her. "How much of your decision is personal and how much is business?"

"It's mostly personal."

"Is 'mostly' fifty-one percent or more than that?"

She sat a little taller, prepared to hear him tell her she had to go after he heard her honest answer. "Closer to ninety-five percent."

He looked more serious than he ever had. "You know marriage will never be part of the equation with me."

"I know."

"Do you really? I don't mean this to come across as egotistical, but I see the way you look at me. I know that women think they can change a man's mind. Mine's set."

He was standing right in front of her now, his gaze not wavering from hers. "Okay."

"Okay what?"

"Your mind is set." The words dragged painfully along her throat. It wasn't what she wanted to hear, but it was better that she knew the truth. And maybe, just maybe, she could change his mind.

"I've had a good time, Victoria."

"Me, too." Her heart began to ache. She wanted—no, needed—this extra week with him, even if she left with a broken heart.

His kiss wasn't soft or tender, but flatteringly uncontrolled. She gave it back to him and took more for herself. He wrenched open her shirt, taking only a second to admire her hot-pink bra before he had her naked from the waist up, his hands and mouth busy until her breasts felt heavy and her nipples hard. He managed to get her jeans down to her ankles, then unzipped his own and joined with her in a powerful thrust. The planes and angles of his face were sharply defined, his mouth a serious line, his jaw like iron as he slipped his hand between their bodies and brought her up fast and hard. He pulled her close as he reached climax at the same time, their bodies one, their satisfaction mutual.

In the quiet aftermath, they held each other until their breathing quieted and slowed. Only the sound of the dogs barking, indicating someone was probably arriving, got them moving. He shoved his shirt in his pants, kissed her hard, then picked up her cell phone from the bench and put it in her hand.

"Call your parents," he said. He grabbed his hat on the way out.

She scrambled to get dressed, although she wouldn't go out into the yard unless he came and got her. She took a deep, shaky breath and dialed her mother.

"Hi, sugar," her mother said. "I was just about to call you. What time does your flight arrive tomorrow? We'll pick you up."

"I've decided to stay another week." Victoria's pulse was pounding in her ears. "I got involved in a project here and I want to see it through."

"You have a job, Victoria. People are counting on you. Hold on. What, James? Yes, it's your daughter. She's not coming home."

"Victoria," her father said a second later. "What's this nonsense?"

"I need one more week, Dad. I'm helping someone get a business started."

"Your cowboy?"

"He's not my cowboy. He's a very talented artist. I'm helping him develop a web presence." Emotion crept into her voice. "He saved my life, Dad. I wouldn't be here if it weren't for him."

A long stretch of silence followed. When he spoke again, he'd lost his irritated tone. "All right, sweetheart. I understand. But one more week is it. You're putting a lot of extra work on your brother."

"Count on me for Sunday brunch," she said.

"I'll send the jet Saturday afternoon," he said, making sure she'd come home.

"Sunday morning."

"Saturday night," he said. She didn't argue.

Victoria pushed the off button and cradled her phone against her chest.

"You played the he-saved-my-life card," Garrett said from the doorway, startling her.

"It was the only reason that would work with him."

"But is that how you feel? You're not doing this… You're not here now because of what happened at the airport?"

"That was originally why I came, but it's not why I stayed. Who's here?" she asked, changing the subject.

"Estelle's son Jimmy. She asked me this morning if I might have part-time work for him. He's nineteen and going to college, studying to be a vet. Knows horses. I figure whatever plan you're making, it'll include having to hire some help."

"It's the only way you can increase your time in the shop." *Unless you take me on permanently.*

"Well, then, come talk to him with me and see what you think."

They found him hanging over the stall of the most skittish horse, talking in a soothing voice. Garrett wondered if that was how he sounded, like a new father trying to calm a crying baby. Victoria went up beside him and introduced herself.

So. She was staying for another week. He'd been geared up for her taking off tomorrow. This change of plans was a blow to his self-control, as evidenced by the way he'd made love to her in the workroom. He was still a little shocked he'd done that in the middle of the day. It was damned satisfying, too, the way she wanted it as much as he did. The way she was ready so fast, as if she'd been thinking about it already.

As she talked to Jimmy, Garrett studied her. He could look at her naked forever. She hadn't worn anything to bed the whole week, even though he'd told her it wouldn't bother him if she did. She said she was surprised at how good it felt not to get tangled up in anything—except him, she'd added, slipping a leg between his.

She was a pretty good cook, too. Better than he was, although she didn't know the first thing about barbecuing steaks. She never seemed bored in the evening, never complained about how dirty the work was taking care of the animals. He did notice she looked at her fingernails now and then with a little yearning glance, and he hadn't seen her hair not in a braid all week. He missed the dark curtain it had made when she was on top, how it cocooned them in their own private world.

She'd already turned his world upside down. After one more week with her, would he be able to right it again? Would she stay in touch because of the business? Would she come back to visit now and then—and expect to share a bed again?

Could he handle that?

That night he showered with her, shampooing her hair then towel drying it after. She'd brought her own products when she moved in, so her hair smelled exotic to him now, not the same as his. She wore a short silk robe that looked completely out of place in his humble home as he brushed her hair, drawing sounds of pleasure from her the whole time.

After a while, he lowered her robe and massaged her back, tracing her spine, bone by bone, her body so incredibly delicate and yet so strong, getting stronger every day.

She wasn't a princess. His expectations had been all wrong. Maybe she was used to the good life, an easy life, but she carried her own weight on his ranch, worked hard and without complaint.

What had she told him before? "You don't have to be what people expect you to be." She wasn't. And for years he'd been doing exactly that himself—living up to expectation. Not showing everyone how much he'd changed, preferring to be alone rather than trying to change people's minds about him.

Maybe they'd changed their minds on their own,

however. No one seemed afraid of him. No one crossed the street rather than walk past him like they'd done years ago.

He knew he hadn't been that person for a long time, but who else did? A few. The vet. Estelle, probably. Other merchants he did business with.

Victoria—although her view of him was from behind rose-colored glasses. He knew he was still her hero. He hadn't done anything, intentional or otherwise, to change her mind about that. As she'd said, they hadn't argued. Their many, many differences hadn't come into play much during the week, probably because they were both blinded by passion. He hadn't felt so much older or less educated. He'd stopped thinking of her as being short, but enjoyed the way he could tuck her under his chin and hold her there.

Knowing they had another week, he could slow down a bit, figure her out more.

Or maybe he needed to speed things up. He was struck by the feeling that something was going to happen to take it all away.

"You have the best hands," she said with a sigh, bringing him back to reality. It would have to do for now.

Chapter Ten

At the sound of a car coming up the driveway several days later, Victoria hurried the final two steps into the barn. She'd helped feed the animals, then had showered and spent the morning in the house making phone calls, but had taken a break to bring Garrett some iced tea. She set down the glass as he emerged from the workroom to look out of the open barn door.

"Looks like your cousin Wendy's car," he said.

Victoria peered out, too. "It is. I hope everything's okay." She stepped into the yard as Wendy parked. Emily sat beside her. They both waved.

"Until you got here, it was rare for anyone other than the vet or Lenny to come by, and that's only business," Garrett said.

"Your point is?"

He gave her a look teetering between humor and exasperation. "It's just an observation."

"Well, when I've gone home, you'll have your peace back." *And how do you feel about that?* she wanted to ask. Every day they were becoming more of a team, the rhythms of doing barn and household chores a routine now. She did get a little lonely for her girlfriends and a little frustrated with the drive into town when she wanted to buy something, she admitted that. It was a huge change for her. But she had so much to make up for it.

"We brought MaryAnne," Wendy said, hugging Victoria. "She's been cleared to appear in public. Hi, Garrett. I haven't seen you in ages." She hugged him, as well.

"Since before you gave birth," he said. "Are you going back to work at Red?"

"Part-time."

Emily got the baby out of her carrier. MaryAnne was awake and alert.

"Nice to see you again," Emily said to Garrett.

"Same here." He touched his hat. "I'll leave you all to talk."

"We brought lunch," Wendy said. "Enough for everyone."

Victoria left the decision up to him, not wanting to push him into socializing.

"I'm sure Victoria would like to spend time just with you, but thanks."

"We'll leave you a plate," Wendy said as he

strolled away. He acknowledged her words with a raised hand.

"I can bring another chair onto the porch," Victoria said, happy to spend time with her cousins.

"Can't we eat inside?" Emily asked. "What?" she said when Wendy made a noise. "I'm dying to see the place Vicki can't seem to quit. Aren't you?"

"I'm curious."

Victoria hoped Garrett didn't think she was taking over, making his house hers. She didn't figure he was embarrassed or anything, but it was his personal space. People sometimes got uptight about such things.

They moved the party inside. As Victoria got out plates for the sandwiches and coleslaw, Wendy and Emily explored.

"Very quaint," Emily said, passing the baby to Wendy. "Manly."

"It suits him," Victoria said.

"At least he has internet and satellite TV."

"A thoroughly modern man," Victoria said, smiling.

"Is he?"

"About some things. Most things, actually," she said after thinking about it.

"Is the couch comfortable?"

"It is."

"To sleep on?"

Victoria ignored the question and took a bite of a chicken sandwich layered with pancetta, sun-dried tomatoes, arugula and parmesan shavings. "This is incredible, Wendy. Is it from Red?"

"No. Just a recipe that looked good."

"Come on, Vicki. Give us a little dirt," Emily said. "Is he good?"

"I'm still here, aren't I?"

"Which is one of the things we came to tell you," Wendy said. "We've been fielding calls from your mother."

"Really? I talk to her every day." She took another bite as she figured out what else to say. She wanted to keep the extent of her feelings for Garrett to herself. The last thing she wanted was for people in town to change their opinion of him because of anything she said or did. "She understands why I've stayed. Dad, too."

Or so they'd said, although her mother had commented in her often cryptic way, "A mother knows every nuance of her child, Victoria. Her voice, her demeanor, even her laughter. You'll see for yourself someday."

"We just thought we'd give you a heads-up," Wendy said. "There's also been a little talk around town. Just a little," she added in a hurry. "Nothing bad, but even though you haven't been flashy about it, your daily presence here has been noticed."

Victoria groaned. He was never going to forgive her for that. "The last thing I want is for his reputation to suffer because of me."

The sisters exchanged glances. "Well, actually, it's improved because of you."

"Seriously? That's good, then." Although she couldn't tell him that. It would sound egotistical.

"Maybe," Emily said hesitantly. "But maybe it's going to cause him problems when you leave. You know, like he wasn't a good guy, after all. There'll be gossip."

Appalled, Victoria dropped her chin to her chest. Once again, her good intentions had taken a wrong turn. She shoved her plate forward a little, planted her elbows on the table and looked out the window at his property. She'd been envisioning a new structure, a huge shelter with lots of dog runs and places to train them. Several areas to quarantine new animals until they passed their vet checks. She'd been thinking maybe he could teach obedience classes, too. He had such an easy way about him.

And now look what she'd done—wreaked havoc for him every step of the way. He would think she was a jinx, that anything she touched turned sour. How could she overcome that?

"Um, we need to talk to you about something else," Wendy said.

"There's *more?*"

"Not about Garrett," Emily said. "We need reassurance that Jordana is okay, Vicki. I know you told us a few weeks ago, but according to everyone at home, she's been taking a lot of sick days or coming in late to work. She isn't showing up for family events, and you know how much she loves them."

"Well, maybe you should finally go home and

check her out for yourself," Victoria fired back, tired of keeping Jordana's secret. After a few seconds of shocked silence, Victoria blew out a breath and said more calmly, "She's not sick. Does she have something on her mind? Yes. She's at a crossroads just like I am. While I have to put up with you because I'm here, she has the luxury of privacy." She flashed a smile.

"I guess I understand that, but she's never left us in the dark before," Wendy said.

Victoria picked up her fork and took a bite of coleslaw, but her appetite was gone. She had to figure out how not to hurt Garrett with her actions. She had to figure out how to keep Jordana's secret when Victoria didn't believe in keeping the pregnancy from the father. Jordana and Tanner needed to talk and reach decisions, and soon.

"May I hold MaryAnne?" she asked Wendy, giving up on eating.

"Not hungry?"

"We had a big breakfast. It's delicious. I'll finish it later." She lifted the baby out of Wendy's arms and sat back in her chair again. "We can go out to the porch and rock when you're done eating."

"Go now, if you want," Wendy said. "We'll finish up and stow the leftovers."

"Okay." Victoria wanted a few minutes to herself, anyway.

The weather was a perfect seventy-five degrees with a slight breeze, but not enough to stir up dust. MaryAnne stared at Victoria, which made her regret not having spent more time with her. After all this time, she should be seeing a familiar face, not that of a near stranger.

She started to fuss. "No. Oh, no, don't do that," Victoria said, jostling her, which only turned her fussing into crying. Her cousins were probably having a big laugh at her expense about now, since neither of them bothered to come outside and help.

"What'd you do to her?" Garrett asked, climbing the porch steps.

She'd never been so happy to see someone. "Nothing! I was just holding her. Shh, baby. Shh."

"Is she hungry?"

"How would I know?"

"Need her diaper changed?"

Victoria lifted her up and sniffed. "I don't think so."

Garrett sat in the second rocker, enjoying seeing Victoria out of her element. *Competent* was usually her middle name.

"You seem to know a lot about babies," Victoria said, her expression one of bewilderment. "You take her."

"Can't. I've been working with the animals too much."

"Go shower and change."

He laughed. "Try a different position. Put her on your shoulder."

That only made things worse.

"Hold her in front of you, her legs against your stomach, then bounce her, using your arms," he suggested. He'd never pictured Victoria with a baby. Himself, either, for that matter, and yet he wanted to cradle the crying infant, to soothe her.

"It's working," Victoria said, relief in her voice and body language. "She's not crying. You're a genius."

"Not much different from soothing a scared animal."

MaryAnne turned toward Garrett, her fists tucked under her chin. He took off his hat. She seemed to study every part of his face. She was probably used to being with women most of the time. His voice was so much deeper, like her father's.

"She's a pretty little thing," he said.

"When she's not crying."

He smiled. "You haven't spent much time with babies, I guess."

"Well, I didn't earn a merit badge in babysitting. Man. My arms are getting tired. She's heavier than she looks."

"Lay her down in your lap. Maybe she's just tired of being held. Maybe she needs a little freedom to move."

He watched Victoria carefully place MaryAnne on her legs, itching to pick up the baby himself. His thighs were longer, would provide a better, more secure cradle.

He looked away then, surprised at his thoughts, which were definitely a first for him. Then a movement caught his eye. Wendy and Emily were peeking out the living room window, watching them.

"We have an audience," he whispered.

Victoria jerked her head toward the window and stuck out her tongue.

They retaliated with funny faces in return until Victoria cracked up.

"You've missed them," Garrett said, enjoying seeing this side of her.

"We've always been close, but even more so as adults. Wendy's only two years younger, so I've been closest to her. It's been hard for me having her move away."

The sisters came out the door, laughing like kids, making him wonder what kinds of gestures they'd been making through the window after he'd turned away. He didn't have a sibling, or even a cousin that he knew of, didn't have that kind of relationship with anyone. He'd made a friend in the army, one who'd helped him get through the long days, made longer by never getting a letter or package from home. Then on the oil rig, an old-timer named Ned had become his mentor, not just about the job but life. Ned had died a few years back.

Garrett only saw his mother if he went to San Antonio with the sole purpose of seeing her. She never contacted him. He'd never known what having a close family meant until he listened to Victoria talk fondly about her brothers and cousins. What would that be like, having someone who mattered for your entire life? Someone who had some of the same memories as you?

He figured Wendy and Marcos would give Mary-Anne more siblings. They each had four of their own. She would have lifelong connections. Lucky girl.

A hand waved in front of his face. "You in there?" Emily asked. "We must be boring the heck out of you."

"Maybe if we'd been neighing or woofing, he would've been paying attention," Wendy said, a teasing glint in her eyes. "Garrett, Marcos asked me to tell you that a man's been asking questions about you around town. It sounds like he's interested in your animal interests."

"I hope it's not another reporter. What'd he look like, do you know?"

"Marcos said he was short and wiry, and he wore a Resistol that was too big for his head."

The description screamed outsider to Garrett.

MaryAnne started to fuss again. "Guess that's our cue to leave. It's too early for her to eat. Maybe riding in the car will soothe her."

She picked up her daughter, said goodbye then walked to the car. Victoria followed, talking to Wendy as she buckled the baby in her carrier. Emily remained behind, watching them.

"Do you believe in destiny, Garrett?" she asked.

Not until recently. He didn't say the words, couldn't trust her not to tell Victoria. Besides that, he needed to figure it out for himself. "I guess *you* do."

"I'm not sure. I only know that you happened to be in the right place at the right time to save Vicki's life. I've been hoping destiny would find me, too, but now I've come to realize that I'm going to have to make my own destiny. I don't have time to wait anymore."

"Well, that's crystal clear."

"Sorry. I was mostly thinking out loud." She touched his arm. "Enjoy your final days with my sweet cousin. All good things must come to an end, as they say."

Final days. Talk about bursting a bubble, which was obviously her intention. What had Victoria told her?

After waving her cousins off, Victoria came up the porch steps. "Are you hungry? They brought great sandwiches and coleslaw."

"Maybe in a bit." *Final days.* The words were already starting to haunt him, a countdown to lift-off and an unknown journey. This was Wednesday. They had until Saturday afternoon. How much could happen in those few days?

Not much, he figured. Or possibly too much. He didn't think there would be a happy medium.

Maybe he should give it up to destiny and see where they ended up. It wasn't like him to leave things alone to happen...

No sooner had the women left than a pickup rumbled up the drive. Painted on the door was the name of a feed store on the outskirts of San Antonio.

The driver hopped down, a clipboard in his hand. "Garrett Stone?"

"That's me." He tried to see what was clipped to the board.

"Got a delivery for you."

"I didn't order anything."

"It's okay, Garrett. I was expecting it," Victoria said.

"You know I use Jensen's. It's local."

The driver waited, but not patiently. He tapped his toe and sighed.

"It's a donation," she said. "Just show the man where to drop the bags, please."

As they unloaded bags of pet food, Garrett kept glancing at Victoria, who never met his gaze. He considered how appropriate it was that they'd been brought together by a tornado, because she *was* a tornado. She whirled into lives and disrupted them. He cleaned things up. She instigated. He handled.

"You'll get a monthly donation," she said idly as they watched the driver leave.

"How did you manage that?"

"Made a few phone calls. It's something I'm good at, Garrett, getting people to donate things. It's just the beginning."

He didn't know how he felt about it. "I didn't realize we'd already started the new venture."

"Not officially, but I wanted to show you a little of what I can accomplish."

Another vehicle was coming down the driveway. "My life was so peaceful before."

She had the audacity to grin. "You didn't know what you were missing, huh?"

A small man with a big hat approached. "Howdy. You Garrett Stone?"

"That's me."

"Been hearing about your place. Thought I'd take a look at what you've got, if you don't mind."

"Are you interested in a particular kind of animal?"

"I'm fond of dogs."

"We've got a few," Garrett said, leading the way, his instincts shouting at him. If he was the same man who'd been asking questions in town, he was interested in Garrett personally, and Victoria, not the ranch animals.

He proved it a while later when he said he'd think it over and be back.

"He won't be back," Victoria said.

"No."

"What do you think he really wanted?"

"Don't have a clue. I don't owe any money beyond the usual debts. Nothing from my past is unresolved." He'd memorized the license place. Maybe Cletus would do him a favor and run it.

"I'm really sorry for all these disruptions to your life, Garrett."

He'd gotten kind of used to it now, but he wasn't about to give her the satisfaction of knowing that.

He called Cletus later, explained he was worried because of Victoria. The Fortunes had, well, a fortune. Garrett wanted to make sure she wasn't a target of some kind. She had the protection of family at home.

"P.I. firm outta San Antonio," Cletus said when he called back with the information.

Garrett didn't know whether to relax or not. A P.I. firm wasn't going to kidnap her for a ransom, but he wasn't comfortable, either, having someone snooping around, whether it was because of him or Victoria.

He would step up his usual vigilance. Nothing would happen to Victoria Fortune on his watch.

Chapter Eleven

Victoria waited until Saturday morning to present her plan to Garrett. She could have done so a day earlier, but she didn't want her last night with him to end up with her sleeping on the couch.

They'd had an amazing three days. Jimmy had come to work with the horses, giving Garrett more time in his shop. She felt confident—and worried. It would be a big change for him. She didn't think he adapted well to change, but it was exciting to think about what he could accomplish. That would be her selling point.

Garrett was seated at the kitchen table across from her. She passed him a binder, then opened her matching one.

"The first page shows what the ranch will look

like." She tapped her freshly manicured fingernail on the mechanical drawing of the new structure she thought would be necessary. "This would allow for the barn to be remodeled so that your workroom could be enlarged."

He didn't lift his gaze from the drawing. "Why would I need that?"

"In case you want to hire help at some point to do some of the basic work."

"I can't ever picture letting someone else do work that has my name on it, Victoria. That would be lying."

"You could have apprentices or interns. Lots of businesses do that."

"Not me. My product, my name. Anything else would be dishonest."

"That's fine." She'd figured he would argue that point, so she moved on. There would be time down the road to try to change his mind.

"You'll need a real office space, not just a computer on top of a desk in your second bedroom. It could be set up in the new structure, where there'd be room to have a shipping and receiving station. Streamlining would save costs down the road."

"Where are we coming up with the money for all this?"

"Take a look at page four. You'd be making more profit from your own work, because you'll be working more and charging more. You may think you've been getting a fair price for your work, but I've done a ton of research into it. You could easily double your prices. Plus you'd get donations, like the pet food."

"I don't want or need to be fundraising, Victoria."

"You wouldn't." She took a steadying breath, because this was the tricky part. "I would. Just like I did with the food, only on a bigger scale."

"How could you do that from Atlanta?"

"It would be possible, but it's not what I'm proposing. I'd run it from here."

He finally looked up.

She explained the various ways she would promote his work and the sanctuary and the legal hoops he would need to jump through. The media push via the internet would be all-consuming at first. "I would take on all the business roles. You could just work. I'd not only run your saddle-and-jewelry business but all the things related to the care of the animals, ordering feed, straw, medicines, whatever is needed. You could still work with the animals, but not have the daily responsibility for their upkeep. Again, we'd use interns, apprentices, even volunteers to help. It would free you to do only the work you choose to do, whatever that may be."

He sat back and stared at her, his expression unfathomable. "You would move to Red Rock? Give up your life in Atlanta? For this?" he asked, gesturing to the space around him.

"In a heartbeat." Did she have doubts? Yes. But not enough to stop her from making the move.

"Why?" he asked.

Because I love you. Because I hope that by being in your life all the time, you would come to love me, too. I'm counting on that. "I've told you I haven't been happy at my job. I've found purpose here, doing something that's important. I can be indispensable, not just a cog in a wheel. I've never wanted anything this much. I'd do a great job for you."

"I don't doubt that." Garrett got up and went to the refrigerator. He grabbed some orange juice and poured himself a glass, stalling.

He couldn't take it all in. He needed time to think about it. The intrusion into his life would've horrified him a few weeks ago, maybe even as little as a week ago. Then he would've said no and walked away. Now he was considering it. That was a shock in itself.

But a crucial question needed to be answered first. "How could I afford you?" It would no longer be their final days. She wouldn't be gone forever.

"I'd work for room and board for now. I'd sell my condo in Atlanta and use the equity from that. My maternal grandmother left me a trust I'll have access to on my next birthday. It's not huge but it'll help. And I figure I'll form a business of my own and take on clients."

Her workload sounded overwhelming to him. As for him using her trust fund, well, they would deal with that impossibility later. No way. "Wouldn't you have enough to do here without adding other clients?"

"I'm leaving the doors open, that's all. At first this would be all I do."

He studied her, looking for insecurities or doubts. He saw none. "In your mind, does that mean we'll be living together? Sharing a bed? Being a couple?" he asked.

"That would be my choice, yes."

"You'd stay without marriage? Because that's not something I can ever offer you." At some point, he would disappoint her. It'd always been so. Or maybe she'd even disappoint him. He was already breaking his rules for her.

She came up and wrapped her arms around him, burrowing close. "I know."

And when you tire of that kind of relationship, what then? he thought. "I see your vision, Victoria. You want bigger and better. I don't know that I do."

She started to argue. He put up a hand. "But I'm willing to give it a shot."

Her arms tightened. When she finally leaned back, he could see the happiness in her eyes.

"Thank you," she said. "It'll be good. You'll see."

He kissed her. It felt different somehow, as if sealing an agreement.

"Now for the hard part," she said, not leaving his arms.

"That was *easy?*"

"A snap." She grinned. "I need you to come home with me tonight and meet my parents. Let them get to know you. I need to explain why I'm leaving the

family business and why I'm joining forces with
you. Meeting you in person will help."

He understood her reasoning. He also knew it
would be an uphill battle. A father didn't take well
to a man taking his little girl away, especially when
that man lived a thousand miles from home, wasn't
college educated, had some jail time under his belt,
didn't have many friends, much less a social circle,
and could not provide a lot of extras in life. Not yet,
anyway.

But then, that was thinking like he was a potential husband when he was only a potential business
partner. Would her parents acknowledge the difference?

"What do I need to wear to meet your king and
queen?" he asked.

She actually squealed as she leaped up on him.
He caught her and held her tight.

"You must own one pair of dress pants," she said.
"If not, you have time to shop."

He set her down. "I am that civilized, yes."

"And the bolo you wore when you rescued me.
It'll bring good luck."

"Fine. But you need to do something for me."

"Anything."

"If you want your parents to believe this is only
a business deal, a partnership in the making, you
need to not look at me like you always do."

She smiled. "And how is that?"

"As if I single-handedly saved the world instead

of one woman. They'll think I'm taking advantage of you."

"Oh, but you have." She toyed with the buttons on his shirt as she spoke, sidling closer. "In wonderful, satisfying ways."

He wouldn't have to give her up. Give this up. His bed wouldn't be empty. He'd been awake most of last night thinking about it. For the past week he'd been secretly creating a bolo tie for her as a going-away gift. He could save it for another occasion now. Something special.

"Same goes for you," he said.

She looked pleased with his answer. "I'll accept all the blame, if that makes you happy, cowboy."

He was afraid to feel happy, wasn't really sure what all it entailed. He only knew he'd felt different since she'd come into his life.

Her cell phone rang. He reached into her back pocket, pulled it out and passed it to her.

"Hey, Em," she said. "Six o'clock. Why?"

Garrett went back to the kitchen table and thumbed through the rest of her plan. Even without studying it, he could see it was ambitious.

"Emily's hitching a ride with us on the jet," Victoria said, coming up beside him. "She decided she should give Wendy and Marcos a few days alone. It's about time."

"She said something cryptic the other day. Something about making her own destiny."

"I know you'll keep this confidential, so I'll tell you. Emily's been baby-obsessed forever. All she's wanted is to be a mom, and she'll be a great one, for sure. Since she turned thirty, she's decided it's never going to happen the usual way, so she's tried to adopt, which isn't working out, or at least not fast enough. Now she's going to register at a fertility clinic. I think that's why she's going home. There's an excellent facility in Atlanta. I also think she wants to check on Jordana for herself."

"What's wrong with Jordana?"

"She's pregnant with Tanner Redmond's baby."

Garrett took a step back, which made Victoria laugh.

"Now you know the family secrets that I've been having to keep. Whew. Sharing that felt good. I haven't been able to confide in anyone."

He shook his head. Family secrets were new to him, but he knew how important it was to Victoria that she be able to confide in him. "I've got your back, princess. Your secrets are safe with me."

Tears welled in her eyes immediately. "Thank you," she whispered.

He didn't know how to deal with her tears, so he picked up his kitchen phone. "I need to get Jimmy to take care of the place. We'll be back tomorrow, right?"

"Even if we have to hitchhike."

He hesitated before he dialed. "Do you think your parents will disown you over this?"

"I think it may make things tough for a little while, but disown me? Never."

"Will your brothers challenge me to a duel?"

"Honestly, I don't know how they'll react. Shane may even be glad to have me gone. I think it's been hard for him being my boss. I didn't take orders well."

"What a shock." He dialed the number, talked to Jimmy, then went into his bedroom to check his clothes. She wasn't packing much at all, having appropriate clothes at her condo to wear.

He'd seen her family's house online, but he'd been wondering what her condo looked like. She would've chosen it herself, decorated it, made it her home. What kind of information could he glean about her by seeing it? Plenty, he figured.

While he was packing, Victoria lay on the bed, not making a comment unless he asked a question. He was glad she wasn't trying to dress him beyond what she'd already told him. He wanted to make a good impression for her sake. For himself, he was okay with who he was, who he'd become, especially recently. He could stand eye to eye with anyone. What he wore mattered little.

"Have I told you what a fine figure of a man you are?" Victoria said.

"Sort of." She stared at him a lot and touched him constantly, even during the night. Her hands would roam over him, even when she seemed sound asleep, as if she couldn't help herself. He simply enjoyed it.

"You are. Lean and strong. Sexy. I love your shoulders and arms best, I think."

"The better to lift you with, my dear."

"What do you like best about me?"

"The rare times you're humble."

She tossed a pillow at him, pretending fury. He tossed it back, then immediately threw another, but that was all he had on his bed. No frilly decorative pillows for him.

"I like everything about you," he said.

"Everything?"

"Maybe you're a little bossy now and then."

"You don't seem to mind if I take the lead in bed sometimes."

"True."

"Or on the sofa."

He remembered that particular moment fondly. "Also true."

She grabbed his shirt and yanked him down, dragging the tails from his jeans. "Or that time on the washing machine when it was on the spin cycle."

"Stop, stop," he said, caught between laughter and fresh desire. "Uncle. I agree that 'bossy' can be a good quality." He glanced at the bedside clock. "Jimmy will be here in fifteen minutes."

"Which is enough time for me. How about you, cowboy?"

"I think I can manage."

Hours later, they picked up Emily and headed to Red Rock Airport. After Emily climbed out of the truck, Garrett looked at Victoria before she hopped down, too. "You okay?" he asked. She hadn't seemed to balk at flying out from the memory-filled airport, but he wanted to make sure.

"You're here with me. What can go wrong?"

He didn't want her believing that. Didn't want her to think everything would be perfect as long as he was with her. She had to be realistic.

But she leaned over and kissed him so that he couldn't—or maybe wouldn't—contradict her.

"Everything's good," she said.

He wished he could believe that. Instead dread invaded him finally—realism. They'd left their fantasy world at the ranch behind and were facing a big unknown, except that he could pretty well predict what her parents' reaction was going to be. He'd gotten enough hints of how they felt when he'd listened to Victoria's side of the many phone calls.

She would be tested by her parents. *Are you strong enough to stand up for yourself, Victoria? Or will going home remind you of how much you would be giving up?*

Garrett needed the answers to those questions.

Chapter Twelve

Everything looks so sterile, Victoria thought as she and Garrett walked into her condo hours later. Her furnishings and art were contemporary; she'd never been a frills and flowers person. Her mother had been taken aback at the way Victoria had furnished her condo, had offered pieces from Victoria's late grandmother's estate, which were in storage. None of them had appealed. Now she could see their value.

"Great view," Garrett said, noticeably not commenting on her condo. He laid his suit bag over the streamlined sofa and moved toward the window. The sky was almost dark, so the skyline was lighting up.

"That's the main reason I chose this place. That

and the in-building gym, so I wouldn't have to go somewhere else to work out. There was a unit available on the third floor, but the fifteenth suited me. Are you hungry?"

"I could eat."

She took a binder out of a kitchen drawer and passed it to him. "What're you in the mood for?"

"What's this?"

"Menus of every place nearby that delivers. I haven't been home for three weeks. Cupboards are bare." She felt uncomfortable around him, showing him the way she lived, the granite countertops, cherrywood cabinets and stainless-steel appliances. The brown leather sofa that held center stage on the hardwood floors.

There was no softness, except a few throw pillows and a shag area rug.

"Let's go out," Garrett said, closing the binder. "We've never been to a restaurant together."

"We've been to Estelle's and Red."

"But we didn't really go together, did we? So, what's your favorite place?"

She came up to him. "We won't run into anyone you know, but we could run into people I know. Are you okay with that?"

"I am if you are." There was challenge in his eyes, as if daring her.

"Garrett, I'm happy to take you anywhere."

"Okay, then. You choose, princess."

He'd almost stopped calling her that. She hadn't missed it.

"Do you dance?" she asked.

"I'm somewhat competent."

"Then I know just the place. Wanna see my bedroom first?" She waggled her eyebrows.

"Sure." He grabbed his suit bag and followed her into her bedroom, which was a little more feminine but still uncluttered and without a floral print in sight.

"I wouldn't have pegged you as a minimalist," he said, looking around. "I never would've walked into this place and thought it was yours."

"It isn't anymore. This belonged to an entirely different person." Her comforter was sage-green. Other than that, there was little color. She watched him open her closet door and hang up his clothes.

"There's color in here," he said. "Lots of shine and glitter, too." He whistled long and low. "Look at all those shoes."

She'd had the closet customized for her. She did like shoes—and purses. She dressed up a lot, too. It was part of how she lived, how she was raised and what people expected of her.

He pulled a garment off the rod and held it up. "Where'd you wear this?"

It was white, strapless and designer. "My debutante ball."

"Debutante," he repeated quietly. "How about this one?"

It was stuck way back in the closet, a yellow, full-skirted, off-the-shoulder number. "One of six bridesmaid gowns. My mom is storing the others in my old bedroom. This one was from a wedding in March. I hadn't taken it to my parents' house yet."

"You live a fascinating life, Victoria."

She couldn't read his thoughts. Didn't have a clue what he was thinking. He was a fish out of water here in her space—and she felt like one now, too.

Suddenly he grinned, moved in on her and backed her to the bed, making her fall onto it, following her down. "At least your bed's a good size. We'll make good use of it later."

Her fears that he was discovering a woman he no longer liked were allayed. He'd just been, well, surprised, probably. Taken aback. He'd found his bearings again.

They didn't linger on the bed but headed out to a club a few blocks away, one that showcased a new band every week. Sometimes it was hard rock, sometimes rhythm and blues, rarely jazz and occasionally country. They got lucky tonight with a local country band, so she figured Garrett would be happy.

After weeks of a steady diet of country music in his house and workshop, she'd developed a feel for it, too, especially the songs that told a story.

For dinner they shared a platter of ribs, corn on the cob and potato salad. Then they danced it off. He taught her a simple line dance and tried unsuccessfully to teach her a more complicated two-step. But when a ballad started, she knew exactly what to do. She moved into his arms, laid her head against his chest and closed her eyes. The dance floor was so crowded, they barely moved their feet. *Foreplay at its finest,* she thought.

"Someone is staring at us," Garrett said, dipping low to whisper in her ear.

"What does she look like?"

"He."

"Move us around so I face him." In a moment she saw who he meant. "That's my brother Shane. When the song's over we can head back to the table. He'll follow. I'm not missing out on a second of this dance."

Garrett didn't want to miss out on anything, either. He didn't know why they hadn't danced before, except it hadn't entered his mind. He would make sure they did from time to time at home, now that he remembered how it could feel.

If she came home with him.

He was beginning to have some doubts about that. He'd taken one step into her condo and realized they were going to face some issues he didn't think had occurred to her. There was lot for her to leave behind.

She was right about her brother. He slid into the booth next to her as soon as they settled in.

"Welcome home, Vick." He held out a hand to Garrett. "Shane Fortune."

"Garrett Stone." He decided to let them lead the conversation. Victoria didn't look at all uncomfortable. In fact, she was grinning at her brother as if challenging him to ask whatever questions were on his mind. Apparently she wasn't going to volunteer information, either.

"So you're home," Shane said.

"A couple hours ago." She took a long swig of water, and her eyes sparkled over the rim.

"You must be her cowboy," Shane said to Garrett. "The reason my workload doubled the past few weeks."

"Mine halved. Sorry," Garrett said with a shrug.

Victoria laughed. "He's my hero, Shane. Be nice."

"We all do appreciate what you did, Garrett. I know I'd sure miss doing this." Shane grabbed her in a headlock and knuckled her scalp until she hollered for him to stop.

"Fortunately, he doesn't do that at the office," she said. "I really am sorry I left you with all the work, but the time away did me a world of good."

"I can see that. You look rested again. Happy. It's been months since I've seen that." He glanced at Garrett. "I guess that's your doing."

"With help from some puppies named Dee and Dum," Victoria answered. "And a dog named Abel, among others. I've found that mucking stalls is good for the soul, too."

"Mucking stalls? You?" Shane said to Victoria. "The original I-can't-stand-dirt-under-my-fingernails girl?"

Which confirmed Garrett's city-girl suspicion about her. "She got herself covered in mud in a storm to save the puppy named Dum. Head-to-toe mud."

Shane eyed her more seriously. "You did?"

She shrugged. "I couldn't let him die, could I?"

"No." He caught a server's attention and asked for a beer, then ordered another one for Garrett.

"Are you here alone?" Victoria asked.

"Nope. Marnie's in the restroom, but she's always there a good fifteen minutes. Why do women take so long?"

"Is she with a girlfriend?"

"Yes. Oh. Right. They've got to analyze the evening so far."

"We enjoy it."

"I take it you haven't seen Mom and Dad yet."

"Tomorrow morning."

"You'll be joining us for brunch?" Shane asked Garrett.

"That's the plan."

Garrett couldn't interpret Shane's expression, something between "Good luck" and "Is your estate in order?" Neither was good.

"There you are!" A curvy blonde came up beside Shane. "We didn't know where you went, sugar."

Shane introduced everyone as he stood. The server showed up at the same time with the beer order so that a bit of chaos ensued, then Garrett and Victoria were alone.

"See you tomorrow," Victoria had said.

"Wouldn't miss it for the world," Shane had answered.

"That was interesting," Garrett said. "Will he warn your parents that I came with you?"

"Oh, no. He loves drama. He'll want to see it unfold. I figure we can show up fifteen minutes before the others usually arrive. That'll get the initial introduction and Q and As over."

The gap between her world and his continued to widen. There was only one place where their world didn't matter, and he wanted to go there right now.

He reached across the table and grabbed her hand. "I have a hankerin' to make love to you."

"A hankerin', hmm? Well, cowboy, I'm all yours."

In her dark bedroom a while later he could imagine they were at his house, in his bed—except that the bed felt different, the room smelled different and it was completely quiet. No puppies whined from their box in the kitchen; no wind blew. He didn't have to keep an ear open for anything unusual happening.

It should've been a vacation for him, but it only made him more anxious to get home.

Victoria made a sleepy sound next to him. He maneuvered her closer, wrapped her in his arms and tried to sleep. He had the terrifying feeling he'd seen his last sunset, eaten his last meal, made love for the last time….

If the I'm-glad-I'm-not-you look in Shane's eyes was any indicator, that is, and Garrett figured Shane knew his parents well. They were a tight-knit family. Shane didn't even know Victoria planned to move to Red Rock, and he was worried for her. All her life she would've been expected to bring home someone suitable. Even her job at JMF was secondary to her job of finding a suitable husband.

Garrett had little hope that the Fortune family would find him suitable.

He turned toward Victoria, heard the steady rhythm of her breathing as she slept.

"I love you," he whispered into her hair, the first-time-ever-spoken words freeing him of every question in his mind about the mixed emotions he'd been experiencing. He couldn't tell her, however, couldn't let that influence her choices. She had to decide what she could live with.

Or without.

Victoria didn't ring the bell on her parents' door. She opened it and went right inside.

"You don't even knock?" Garrett asked. Forget the internet. In person it was even grander. It seemed like a place where one should knock, like a uniformed butler would come to the door.

"I never do, so if I did today they would know something was up."

"I'm not invisible, princess."

She smiled, although it was shaky. He wished he could hold her hand, not only to settle her but himself.

"I'm home!" Victoria called out.

"You're early," her mother said, coming up a long hallway. "I—" She slowed upon seeing Garrett. Victoria's father came out of his den at the same time.

"Mom, Dad, I'd like you to meet Garrett Stone. Garrett, this is James and Clara Fortune."

Because civility was rooted deeply, her parents welcomed him politely, this king and queen who reigned supreme in the family.

"Welcome to our home, Mr. Stone," her father said.

"Garrett, please."

James nodded, but didn't offer the same in return.

"Coffee's ready," Clara said. "Shall we go into the living room?"

A coffee service was set up. At least there were mugs, not cups and saucers, Garrett thought, although the mugs were more dainty than he was comfortable with.

"I'll get yours," Victoria said to him, indicating he should sit on a love seat nearby.

"None for me, thanks." He remained standing. He was a man of action, didn't like putting off anything, even those things that might cause discomfort. He wanted to get it over with.

She gave him a curious look, poured for herself and her mother, then sat on the love seat. Clara settled in a delicate chair. James also refused coffee and didn't sit. They looked like a snapshot out of an Agatha Christie play, intrigue abounding in an elegant drawing room.

"We should have thanked you long ago for saving our girl's life," James said. "We can't thank you enough."

"Right time, right place," he said, tired of all the gratitude. It'd been destiny, just as Emily said.

"So, why have you come here with my daughter?"

"I wanted you to meet him," Victoria said before Garrett could answer. "I also wanted to let you know in person that I'm quitting my job at JMF and going to work for Garrett."

"In Texas?" Clara asked, sounding surprised and resigned at the same time.

"In Red Rock, yes, ma'am."

Garrett heard a tiny quaver in Victoria's voice. Her eyes had gone wider, too, her back stiffer. In fact, her posture had been different from the moment they stepped inside the house. She set her mug aside. It rattled against the coaster for a second.

"I've never been as excited about working on a project as I have been these past few weeks. I need to be part of the completion."

"And is Garrett part of being excited about it?" James asked, as if Garrett weren't in the room.

"Of course. There wouldn't be a project without him. Daddy, we're going to build an animal sanctuary where—"

"Will you be living with him?" her father continued.

"Yes, sir."

"Sharing a bedroom, as you have been for a while now?"

"How do you know that?" Victoria asked.

Garrett had eased over to where Victoria sat. "He

hired a private investigator to look into me," he said, keeping his voice steady and polite. "It's all right, Victoria. I would've done the same thing in his position. Fathers protect daughters."

"I had to be sure. Marry a Fortune and you marry the Fortune family."

"We haven't mentioned marriage," Victoria said. "We're entering into a business deal. That's all. Please give Garrett a chance. Please get to know him. I know you'll come to like and admire him as I do."

James focused on Garrett then. "I'm all ears. What do you have to say, Mr. Stone?"

Garrett realized he'd been kidding himself. He couldn't take her from this life, this world. It was just a fairy tale to her. He could see the future clearly, and she couldn't. She didn't have enough life experience. Once the excitement wore off, it would be tedium to her, and she might not be willing to tell him that she'd made a mistake. Not too many women would be happy living his kind of life.

More important, he couldn't be party to creating a rift between her and her family, be the cause of their disapproval and disappointment. He'd lived with his mother's disappointment his whole life. He knew what that was like.

He turned to Victoria and said what needed saying, not taking the chance of going somewhere private to have a discussion. He'd been losing discussions with her. He couldn't lose this one.

"This isn't going to work," he said. "I'm sorry,

Victoria. I can't do this." He gave a slight bow to her parents and took long strides across the room, then the foyer, then out the door. He didn't look back, not even when she called his name.

He never should have stopped trusting his instincts.

Victoria rushed to the window and watched him walk away. They didn't live on a bus line. He didn't have a cell phone to call a cab. What was he going to do?

"He's gone. Are you happy now?" she almost yelled.

"If it takes so little for him to give up," her father said calmly, "then you're better off without him. You need a real man."

"A real man?" She flung her arms up. "What does that mean to you? Because to me a real man is one who fulfills his responsibilities, keeps his word, protects those who need protecting, doesn't complain about working hard so that others can be more comfortable, whether they're human or animal. A real man cares more about others than himself. He does an honest day's work. He lives by a code he sticks to, come hell or high water.

"You know what he told me? He said he doesn't need bigger and better, but that I do. Maybe he's right. Maybe I came up with this plan because I wanted more. I fell in love with him because he's a real man. And he didn't fall in love with me because

I'm not a real woman. I'm spoiled. I'm pampered. I'm not worthy of him."

"Nonsense," her mother said. "You're worthy of anyone in the world. We were ready to accept him, sugar. We found nothing in the investigator's report that would've stopped us from welcoming him."

"If I hadn't approved," her father said, "you would've been home a week ago. He had youthful indiscretions. He paid for those long ago."

"Why didn't you tell him that?" Her heart was breaking. She didn't know who or what to blame. She needed to blame something.

"He didn't give me a chance, now did he?"

"What am I supposed to do now? He was all I wanted. I wanted to marry him." Tears were flowing unchecked. Her mother tucked a tissue in her hand. One wasn't nearly enough.

"Victoria, my dear," her mother said. "The best thing we can do is to marry the man we need, not the one we want."

"What? I don't even know what that means, Mom. Please, I have to go home." She grabbed her purse and raced toward the front door.

Her mother caught up to her as she fumbled with her car keys. "You can't drive in this condition, Victoria. Stay here with us, sugar. Let me take care of you."

"I need to be alone. Please don't call me. I'll get in touch when I'm ready."

"Here come Shane and Wyatt. One of them

can drive you home in your car, and the other can follow. You really shouldn't be on the road."

"I don't want to explain what's going on to anyone else."

"I'll take care of it." Her mother walked up to her sons, said something, then Shane came over and took her keys out of her hand as he urged her toward the passenger seat. Her big brothers had always watched over her. It made her cry again.

"I'm quitting my job. I'll work until you find a replacement."

"We'll talk about it. There's no need to make a hasty decision."

"It's well thought out, Shane, believe me." She didn't know what she would do next, but it wasn't going to be selling retirement plans. She needed to do work with a purpose, something satisfying. She needed to find a job on her own, not be given one.

She got her keys from Shane, thanked both brothers and made the long, lonely elevator ride up fifteen floors. Once she got inside her condo she stood and stared. His suit bag was draped over her couch. They'd planned to fly back tonight but were going to take a cab to the airport so they hadn't loaded their things in her car.

Victoria went straight onto her balcony, flinging the slider open so hard it bounced back. She shoved it then, stepped out, tried to draw enough air to fill her shaky lungs. With the door closed she rarely heard a sound, but now she could hear sirens and a car horn. The air wasn't pure enough, didn't feel clean inside her chest. Abel hadn't greeted her at her front door. She couldn't bury her face in his fur and find comfort there.

She made her way back into her living room, kicking off the high heels that had been hurting all morning. Boots. She wanted her boots.

She unzipped his bag, pulled out his shirt and pressed her face into it, trying to find his scent. After a long while, she picked up the phone.

"Em? Is there any chance you could come over?"

"What's wrong? You sound terrible."

"Remember when you asked if I'd ever been rejected?"

"Yes." The word came out slowly, asking a question at the same time.

"I told you yes, but I really didn't have a clue." Her head ached from so much crying. Her heart compressed into a hot ball of fire. "Now I do."

Chapter Thirteen

"Um, you've recovered?" Emily asked Victoria a few days later. They were sitting on Victoria's balcony enjoying margaritas and the view.

"I have," Victoria said. *Except for the nightmares.*

"So, why haven't I seen you smile once?"

"I'm not saying I've fully recovered, but I'm on my way. Something my mom said helped a lot. She said, 'Marry the man you need, not the one you want.'"

"What does that mean?"

She squeezed Emily's hand. "I'm so glad I wasn't the only one not to understand. It took me a while, but I figured out that we are supposed to marry the man who's good for us, who'll take care of us, who'll provide a good life. He's what we need. But wanting is physical and ephemeral. It doesn't last."

Emily didn't say anything for a while, then finally said, "What if that's not what she means at all? What if she means we're supposed to marry the man who sees us as we are and accepts us as is? Don't we need a man like that more than one who just wants to sleep with us all the time? Of course, in an ideal world, the two combine and life is good."

"Well, of course. Ideal would be good." She had to give it more thought. She'd thought that Garrett did see her as she was, did accept her as is. The wanting was strong, too. But in the end, he hadn't proposed, had even walked away without discussing it with her. He'd also taken away the opportunity to work together, the chance to let love grow.

"Here's an easier question. What are you going to do for work?" Emily asked.

"I don't know yet. I'm exploring my options."

"What do you want to do?"

I want to create the Pete's Retreat Foundation with Garrett. The words popped into her head without a moment's thought. It was what she wanted more than anything.

She wanted to be with the man she needed *and* wanted.

"What are you thinking, Victoria?"

"That it's time for a road trip."

"Where?"

"To Red Rock. Wanna come along?"

"You've been after me to come home, which I

finally did, and now you're trying to get me to go back?"

"We both know you only came home for a visit, and with a specific purpose in mind. As soon as you're inseminated, you'll move to Red Rock. I've decided to live there, too."

"I haven't even started the paperwork at the clinic. And you've lost your mind, Vicki. I think you've had too many margaritas."

"I've had three sips of one."

"Well, it's gone to your head. Why would you go back to the place of such heartache?"

"Because I felt alive there." Which was the tip of the iceberg for her. Yes, a lot of it had to do with Garrett, but a lot didn't.

"What will you do for work?"

"I can commute to San Antonio if I have to. I'll find something, Em. I can't stay here anymore. Too many people. Too many cars." Not enough Garrett.

"Are you going to try to rent this place or sell it?"

"I'm going to cut ties. I'll be home to visit often, but I can stay with any number of family members. So, do you want to come along?"

"When will you leave?"

"Saturday. I can spend the night midway. Where would that be? Jackson, Mississippi, maybe? I'll drive the rest of the way on Sunday."

"I couldn't be ready by then," Emily said. "I can't believe you're doing this."

She needed to end the nightmares again. If she stayed in Atlanta, they would never go away.

She was haunted by visions of Garrett's animals wandering loose or getting caught in storms. She dreamed about him getting hurt with no one there to see, much less be able to help. If only he'd get a cell phone—

"You're going after Garrett again," Emily said, narrowing her eyes.

Victoria shrugged. "We'll be living in the same town, shopping in the same stores, eating in the same restaurants. It'll be hard to avoid him completely."

Emily grabbed her hand. "I don't want to see you hurt again. You haven't even recovered yet, no matter what you say."

"He's worth fighting for."

After Emily left, Victoria called Jordana and made the same offer of a ride to Red Rock.

"No, thank you." Her answer was quick and light. "Drive safe."

"Do you ever plan on telling Tanner?"

"Of course I do."

"Well, maybe you should do it before he gets married to someone else."

There was a brief, tense silence, then, "He's getting married?"

"How would I know? But there's nothing to stop him, is there?"

"That was mean, Vicki."

"It was the truth. Honey, I know you're scared. I would be, too, but you can't wait any longer. Pretty soon your family is going to storm your doors, your secret will be out and they'll force you to tell him. It'll be better if you do it."

Victoria hung up feeling strangely energized. Once she'd made her decision, she had stopped grieving. She had a plan, a goal. She would not live the rest of her life regretting that she hadn't tried hard enough.

She wasn't even nervous about telling her parents.

Four days later, her car packed full and with more to be shipped later, she hit the road, alone, excited and feeling a freedom she'd never felt before. She knew what she wanted. Now she had to go get it.

Red Rock, here I come.

Garrett arrived at Red at his usual time on Sunday night. Marcos looked up from the podium and smiled. One hurdle jumped. At least Marcos wasn't going to shun him for hurting his wife's cousin. Or maybe he didn't know yet.

"How's business?" Garrett asked.

"Can't complain. Thanks for letting me know you'd be in to pick up last week's order tonight."

"I would've paid for it regardless."

"I know. Your usual tonight?"

"Sounds good. No, wait. How about some Carne à la Mexicana instead?"

"Shaking up your life, huh?" Marcos asked.

Is that what he was doing? He headed into the main dining room and bar. The bartender spotted him and started pulling a draft. Garrett had almost reached his usual bar stool when he spotted a woman sitting a few seats down, her shiny brown hair cascading in soft curls down her back. His heart stopped for a couple of beats as he was reminded of Victoria. He didn't even want to sit near the woman.

But then she turned and spotted him. "Well, hello there, cowboy," Victoria said as if nothing had happened between them. "I was hoping I'd run into you tonight." She patted the stool on the other side of her. "I brought your things."

Numb, he took a seat, leaving one chair between them.

"How's it going?" she asked.

"What are you doin' here?"

She'd changed in ways he couldn't define yet. She smiled a kind of a secret smile, like she knew something he didn't. She nodded, too, as if he'd said something she'd been waiting to hear. What the hell was going on?

"I moved here," she said. She might as well have been telling him she was running an errand, something routine and normal, her voice was so calm. This was not normal.

"Why?"

"I'm looking for what I need, not just what I want."

"You are making no sense."

"I came to love Red Rock, so I quit my job, packed my car and here I am."

She sipped some frothy concoction, which left a bit of pink foam on her lips. Rather than use a napkin, she ran her tongue across her lips. She had to know it would drive him crazy.

"A bunch of your stuff is still at my place," he said.

"I know. I'll get it all sometime. Or you can drop them off at the Red Rock Hotel. I've got a room there for now. If Emily moves here—and I don't know that she will—maybe she'll rent a house with me. We'll see what happens."

"Is she pregnant?"

"She hasn't started the process."

"And Jordana?"

"Still hiding out."

Maybe he should give her a call, give her a man's point of view about her keeping that critical information from Tanner. "How do your parents feel about your move?"

"They want me to be happy."

He stared at her painted nails, which reminded him why he'd left her in the first place. "Do you really think you'll find happiness here?"

"This town has felt like home almost since the first day I got here."

He didn't know what to say. It changed everything and nothing. "Have you eaten?" he asked.

"Yes." She stretched and yawned. "And I'm wiped out. I drove four hundred and fifty miles today. I need sleep." She tucked some bills under her glass and climbed off the stool, then slid his suit bag onto the chair next to him.

"Guess I'll be seeing you around town, cowboy." She patted his arm, then looked over his shoulder. "Do you believe in destiny, Garrett?"

"Sometimes."

She looked at him and laughed. "That is so you. Well, in this case, I'm looking at Tanner Redmond, who just walked in." She dug into her purse, pulled out a business card and turned it upside down on the bar. He watched her write Jordana's name and phone number on it.

"Bye, Garrett," she said. She went right up to Tanner, who'd taken a stool at the bar. "You need to call her," she said to the surprised man. "She has something important to tell you."

She held up her hands toward Garrett, her fingers crossed. She was taking a big risk, and the possible unforgiving wrath of her cousin for interfering, but Garrett approved.

After a minute she passed in front of the window and didn't look inside at all. She was over it? Over him? Just like that?

He'd been afraid he'd hurt her, but apparently she'd recovered better than he had.

He sipped his beer, considering her. He'd never known loneliness. Even though he'd spent most of his life alone, he never would've called himself lonely.

And he wasn't lonely now, he decided…

No, he was forlorn. And desolate.

Marcos set his hot plate on the counter in front of him.

"You might have mentioned that Victoria was here," Garrett said.

"I didn't know it mattered." He smiled grimly and walked away.

Was that the response he would get from everyone in town now? Did everyone know? She'd made herself a welcome part of the community in less than a month. He'd lived here most of his life, and he didn't figure anyone would champion him like that, although Victoria had seemed to from the start, even without knowing the details of what had happened with Jenny Kirkpatrick. After all these years, did he need to explain it? Her family moved away years ago.

When Garrett arrived home later, he went straight to his bedroom and opened the closet door. Her clothes were still hanging there. He'd ignored them all week, even though he knew he should pack them up and ship them to her.

One by one, he took her clothes off the rack. Out of his dresser he withdrew the rest of her things, a rainbow of lacy lingerie he loaded into a paper sack. Her perfume wafted from the bag. He rolled it down and took it to the living room along with her clothes. He would take them all to her tomorrow. Get it over with.

He tripped over her boots when he returned to the bedroom. He'd brought them in from the porch a few days ago, had cleaned and polished them so that he could mail them with her clothes. He'd been methodical and unemotional, doing a job that needed doing.

But he clasped them now as he remembered the way she kicked the dirt when she was getting ready to tease him or tick him off. The way she pitched dirty straw into the wheelbarrow, her feet planted. The way she'd saved Dum, her boots filling up with mud so that she could barely walk.

Indelible memories. And now she'd moved to town. He couldn't escape the memories—or her. She would probably start dating, in time get married and have children. Another man's children.

Garrett threw the boots across the room, rattling an old cross-stitch sampler on the wall that said Home Sweet Home. It had come with the ranch, and he'd never taken it down. The sampler tilted for a second then fell to the floor, the old wooden frame breaking into pieces.

It seemed like an omen—or a sign of what his life had become. No home sweet home for him.

Garrett picked up the four wooden pieces, then the cloth sampler itself, which disintegrated at his touch. Dust must've been holding it together, and now it had turned to dust.

He shoved his hands through his hair, then he went to his shop and got out the bolo he'd created for her from his safe. He set it on the counter, pried out the stone, then threw the silver into a crucible. He could melt it down, reuse it. He didn't want reminders of a farewell gift to her.

He turned the stone over and over in his hand. He needed to do something else with it, something that made a statement.

The idea came to him in a flash of light. He settled in and got to work.

It would be his best work yet.

Chapter Fourteen

"He hasn't even had the courtesy to return my clothes," Victoria complained to Wendy after eating dinner on the sunporch after Marcos went to work. "It's been *days*."

"Maybe he wants you to come to him. Come to the ranch. Victoria, you are bouncing MaryAnne like you're on a trampoline. Please sit down."

Victoria stopped bouncing and looked at the baby in her arms, all wide-eyed and beautiful. "She looks fine to me."

"She's getting green around the gills. You're making her seasick!"

Victoria sat in Wendy's rocking chair. "Why would he want me to go to the ranch?"

She hadn't come up with a clear plan about winning him back, but she knew it had to start with contact, and she thought for sure he would bring her clothes to her at the hotel. Make contact. She'd counted on that.

"I don't know. I'm just trying to think like a man," Wendy said.

"Men like the chase. Are you listening, sweetheart?" Victoria said to MaryAnne. "Don't make yourself too available. They'll drop you like a hot poker."

Wendy threw up her hands. "Will you please not poison my not-yet-three-month-old daughter?"

"You're right. She has plenty of time to learn about heartache on her own."

Wendy rolled her eyes. "So, when you told me you were moving here no matter what happened with Garrett, was it a lie? If you're going to spend years being angry at him, what's the purpose of a new beginning here?"

Which was an excellent question, Victoria decided. "I'm not ready to give up, that's all. I'll adapt when I have to."

"In the meantime, we all have to listen to you moan and gripe?"

"Pretty much, yes."

Wendy laughed, then Victoria joined in.

"So, now what?" Wendy asked.

"I guess I'll go out to the ranch and collect my stuff. I've been feeling like a walking neon sign wearing my Atlanta clothes instead of my jeans and boots."

"Let me know how it goes."

"I will." Victoria kissed MaryAnne's cheeks then passed her to her mother. They'd spent enough time together in the past few days, and without Emily there to hog the baby, that Victoria had started feeling comfortable not just holding her but changing her diaper and getting her in and out of her baby carrier, with all its complicated straps and fasteners.

Dogs were easier, but they wouldn't let her cuddle them for long.

"What are you smiling about?" Wendy asked as they moved toward the front door.

"How incredibly my life has changed in a month. Just one month. Can you believe it?"

"Since the same thing happened to me, I *can* believe it. I hope you have the same happy ending I did."

Victoria debated whether to go back to her hotel room and change into something more alluring than the blouse and slacks she wore or just go straight to the ranch. It would be dark in an hour. She should wait until morning—

No. She needed to get it over with.

The drive seemed incredibly long. She hadn't driven the route in more than a week. As it became more desolate, with fewer houses, she began to question herself. Was she still so sure she wanted this life? Would it satisfy her?

Could she satisfy him? Not in bed, that was easy, but as a partner?

Apparently he didn't think she could. She wanted

the chance to prove him wrong, maybe even prove herself wrong. The niggles of doubt would be settled with time.

She pulled into the driveway. Her heart thundered so loud, she thought it would open her chest. She didn't see his truck, but saw Jimmy's pickup.

Where could Garrett be? He didn't have a regular place to go on Thursday nights.

"Howdy, Victoria," Jimmy said, coming up to her. "I didn't recognize the car, but I guess it's your own, not a rental. Heard you moved to town for good."

Abel shoved his head into her, his tail and hindquarters wagging like crazy. Pete watched, looking somber. "I did. Where's Garrett?"

"He didn't say. He had me come before the crack of dawn. Want me to give him a call?"

She was giving Abel a rubdown that he was thoroughly and noisily enjoying. "If you don't know where he is, how can you call?"

Jimmy grinned. "He got himself a cell phone. Can you believe it?"

No, she couldn't. What did that mean? "It is hard to imagine. Anyway, it's okay. Um, I just came to pick up a few things I left. I'll just go in the house and get them."

"Sure thing. You want to see the animals? I'm about ready to get them bedded down for the night, so now would be the best time. Just put Dee and Dum in the house, in fact."

"Yes, I'd love to."

She kicked up dust as she walked next to Jimmy into the barn. She peeked into the stall with the mama dog and puppies. "Look how they've grown," she exclaimed, tears springing to her eyes. Babies grew so fast. The kittens had their eyes open and were stumbling over each other and their mama. There were a couple of new dogs, a few were gone. Apple Annie held court in her stall, but only one other horse was in residence.

Changes could happen in the blink of an eye.

"Somebody brought a boa constrictor the other day," Jimmy said. "Garrett about threw a conniption fit. I took the snake home with me. Figured I could find it a permanent place somewhere."

She couldn't imagine Garrett throwing a conniption fit over anything. He was patience personified. "That must've been something to see."

Jimmy shrugged. "He's been pretty edgy lately. I didn't know him before I started working here, but I'd heard from my mom that he wasn't one to shift gears real easy, you know? Pretty mellow guy. I haven't always seen that."

"Everybody has problems now and then."

"That's what I figure. He keeps his mouth shut pretty good about stuff, though."

Except when he tells you it isn't gonna work and walks out, she thought.

She headed into the house and reached for the light switch. The room lit up. Dee and Dum started making noises, knowing someone was there.

And right smack in front of her on the sofa were

her jeans and shirts on hangers draped over the back, and a paper sack that probably substituted as a suitcase for her undergarments and toiletries and her boots, polished to such a shine she could see her reflection.

She felt the blow of rejection as hard as she had at her parents' house, maybe harder, because this time she had no doubts whatsoever. She knew she wanted to be his wife, the mother of his children, his partner in everything.

She stood staring at the couch until she was dizzy. She staggered into the kitchen, leaned over the sink and cried. She couldn't go outside and face Jimmy until she got herself under control. He would tell Garrett. She couldn't have that. Garrett only needed to know that she'd gotten her things, and that made it over and done with.

The puppies were whimpering, having seen her. She reached into the box and picked up Dum, who wriggled even more than Abel had. He licked her face until she laughed and cried at the same time, then she tucked him under her chin and felt his soft fur against her neck. She'd missed this so much. All of them. Even the stinky dogs who liked to roll in manure.

The front door opened. "I'm just getting a drink of water," she called out to Jimmy. "I'll be there in a sec."

But Jimmy didn't come into the doorway. Garrett did, and he was all dressed up—or dressed up for him, anyway. It was the same outfit he'd worn when he'd met her parents, although a different bolo. This one had more detail and a large blue stone, maybe a sapphire. He held his black Stetson, turning it in his hands.

"Victoria," he said.

"I got tired of waiting for my clothes." She put Dum back into the box and started past Garrett. "I'll be out of here in a second."

She wanted him in the worst way. He looked good. Really good. Relaxed. How ridiculous was it that she wanted him when he didn't want her at all? Or need her.

He set a hand on her shoulder, blocking her way. "You've been crying."

She didn't look at him. "I hadn't realized how much I missed the animals, you know? When Dum's old enough, maybe I can adopt him. I'm trying to find a house to rent that has a yard. Maybe Abel, too."

"We'll talk about it."

Fresh tears stung her eyes. She hated that he was seeing her so emotional. "You're probably tired from your trip, so I'll get going. Bye, Garrett."

"I'm fine. Don't hurry on my account, Victoria," he said. He tossed his hat onto the sofa, landing it next to her belongings. Usually he was fastidious about hanging it on a rack by the door.

She made a move to go again, then noticed his shirt pocket. "Why did you get a cell phone?" she asked.

"I was feeling too out of touch with the world."

"I thought you liked that."

"Changed my mind. You look good."

It wasn't her imagination. He really was in a happy mood. "I— Um, thank you."

"You're welcome."

"And you're dressed up," she said.

"Would you like something to drink?" he asked as he went into the kitchen. "I've got a powerful thirst."

"I'm okay, thanks. What's going on with you? You're not yourself."

"No, I'm not, am I? I've changed." He grabbed a bottle of water—bottled water, really?—and drank most of it in one gulp, the only indication he wasn't as relaxed as she first thought.

He's nervous, she realized. It steadied her a little.

He finished the water and set down the bottle carefully. Then he said, "This wasn't the way I planned it, but I think destiny's taken hold again."

"Planned what?" Whatever he was about to say would be momentous, that much she knew. *Tell me fast,* she urged him silently.

"I'm dressed up because I flew to Atlanta and back today."

"Why?"

"I needed to pay a visit to the king and queen."

"Why?" she asked breathlessly, afraid to guess the answer.

"I had some explaining to do. Let's go sit on the couch."

With one end of the sofa piled high, they were

forced to sit close to each other. Garrett could've moved everything, but didn't, making sure she wasn't too far away.

"My parents actually let you in the house?" she asked.

"They seem to have accepted the fact you want to be in Red Rock, whether you're with me or not. Your mother, in particular, gets it." In fact, she'd told Garrett that she'd never seen Victoria so happy, especially after months of seeing dark circles under her eyes and a weight loss she couldn't afford. "I took your business plan with me and showed it to your father. He was highly impressed, by the way, and regretted not realizing himself that your talents should've been used better at his company."

"I did a great job because it was personal and important," she said, but she looked pleased at the praise.

"I finally read the whole thing, Victoria. It was amazing, from beginning to end. I made a few notes, though."

She laughed. The sound was shaky, in a good way, a way that said her emotions were involved. "Of course you did."

He opened the folder and showed her the changes he would make.

"So, you're going to do it?" she asked.

He shrugged. "Depends on a few things falling into place." He pulled out a sheet he'd tucked in the back and showed it to her.

She examined it. "This looks like a house."

"It is. It'll be built right in this spot, although it'll take up more room than this one by far. Figure we can live in a mobile home for a little while."

"We? You and me?" Her fingers were linked into a white-knuckled knot. He cradled her hands in his until she opened hers, then he clasped them.

"I asked your father for permission to court you. He gave his blessing. Now I'm asking permission from you. I know I hurt you, Victoria. I'll never forgive myself for that." He stood then, needing to move. "And I need to tell you about Jenny Kirkpatrick, before you give me your answer."

"Is she the source of the scandal?"

"Yes."

"I don't need you to tell me, Garrett. I know the man you are."

"Maybe you do, but you don't know why I fought being with you, why I didn't believe I was good enough. Maybe this will explain it."

"Okay."

He told her the story and discovered the memory no longer hurt.

"Since I was a teenage girl myself once," Victoria said, "I'll wager that she's the one who pursued you, even though you were doing the standup thing when her parents put a stop to things."

"Yeah. No one believed me, and I got tired of justifying it. I joined the army."

"Yet you came back after that."

"I didn't know anything but this place. It was home. When I left the second time and came home,

I'd seen more of the world, knew I could live alone and not be bothered by what people thought. But when it came to you, I cared what people thought. And I've been prejudiced, too. I figured the Fortune family would be just like the Kirkpatricks. I was wrong. I'm eatin' crow, big-time."

She pressed her fingers to her mouth, her eyes welling with tears. "And now you're going to court me?"

"I've been givin' that a lot of thought as I made the trip home." He finally sat beside her again. He took her hands again. "See, your father said I could take it a step further if I wanted. That I had his blessing to ask you to marry me, if I wanted, but I thought I should do the right thing. You know, start from the beginning. Do better."

"I don't see how you could do better, cowboy."

He wanted to kiss her, but he needed to finish what he had to say first. "I told your father not only could I provide for you, but I could provide well. I'm not a poor man, Victoria. Not anywhere near it. You've changed my life in just about every way, from how I think to how I act to how I feel. I'm carin' about things I never cared about before. I'm in love with you, princess. I'd like to have a passel of kids with you. Will you marry me?"

"How many is a passel?" she asked, her eyes going wide.

"More'n a few. I want my kids to have what I didn't—lifetime connections, the bonds of family. Are you game?"

"I love you, cowboy. With all my heart. I'm game for anything with you. Do you know why?"

"Tell me."

"Because you're the man that I need."

He kissed her then, tasted her hot, salty tears, then pulled her into his arms for the longest, hardest hug of his life.

"Your father only asked one thing," he said, not letting her loose. "That you have the wedding you deserve."

She leaned back a little and combed his hair with her fingers. "Do you mind?"

"If it's important to you, I can do anything. Victoria, I've been lost without you here. Utterly lost. I know you need more of a social life than I do, and I'll work on givin' you that."

"You keep dropping *g*'s for me, and I'll be plenty happy."

"Huh?"

"I'll tell you later. Or maybe I won't."

"You've been home for half an hour and you're already teasing me. Wait here a minute." He went outside, was gone less than thirty seconds and returned with a gift bag. First he handed her a framed cross-stitch piece like the one that hung in his bedroom, but without explanation. Then he gave her an envelope with a gift certificate inside for fifty-two manicures. "I had to get Gwen to open up her shop tonight. Every year on our anniversary I'll give you fifty-two more. You need to keep your nails nice. I know it means something to you."

She laughed and kissed him. "I didn't know you were so observant."

"When it comes to you? I notice just about everything." Then he dug into the bag for the final item, a small velvet bag. He reached inside and fished around for a particular piece. "Maybe you noticed I didn't bring your clothes to you, even though you told me I could."

"I was devastated. I thought you never wanted to lay eyes on me again."

"I didn't want to see you until I was done with this." He held up an intricately carved silver ring. Woven into the design was a chocolate diamond. "I got you a chain, too, because I figure you won't want to wear it doing all the dirty work around here."

"Oh, Garrett! It's beautiful! I'd never heard of chocolate diamonds until I met you."

He slid the ring on her finger. "That's one of the things I remembered from the airport, how your eyes looked like these stones." He tipped the rest of the contents of the bag into her hand. "There's two wedding bands." He'd spent the better part of three days creating the three rings.

"Pretty sure of yourself, cowboy."

He almost told her he hadn't been sure at all, but decided she didn't need to know that. "I was hopeful."

"I was hopeful, too."

"Would you really have stayed in Red Rock, even without this?"

"It's home, Garrett. But this is my world, right here. I love you."

"I love you, too." He framed her face with his hands. "Remember a while back when you told me we don't have to be what people expect us to be?"

"I do."

He paused at the words. He would hear her say those words soon, too, and she would legally be his forever. "I realized I'd been doing that, figuring everyone had a certain opinion of me that I was sure I couldn't change. I'm not that uncivilized jerk people thought I was, not anymore. I deserved the title once, but not now."

"I didn't have anything to do with that change, you know," she said, her gaze never wavering. "You'd done it for years before I came along."

"But I didn't know it. You think I saved your life? Well, you saved mine in ways you can't begin to imagine."

"Let's go to bed, cowboy."

"It'd be my pleasure."

* * * * *

THE ANNIVERSARY PARTY

Dear Reader,

I am a big believer in celebrating milestones, and for Special Edition, this is a big one! Thirty years… it hardly seems possible, and yet April 1982 was indeed, yep, thirty years ago! When I walked into the Harlequin offices (only *twenty* years ago, but still), the first books I worked on were Special Edition. I loved the line instantly—for its breadth and its depth, and for its fabulous array of authors, some of whom I've been privileged to work with for twenty years, and some of whom are newer, but no less treasured, friends.

When it came time to plan our thirtieth anniversary celebration, we wanted to give our readers something from the heart—not to mention something from our very beloved April 2012 lineup. So many thanks to RaeAnne Thayne, Christine Rimmer, Susan Crosby, Christyne Butler, Gina Wilkins and Cindy Kirk for their contributions to *The Anniversary Party*. The Morgans, Diana and Frank, are celebrating their thirtieth anniversary along with us. Like us, they've had a great thirty years, and they're looking forward to many more. Like us, though there may be some obstacles along the way, they're getting their happily ever after.

Which is what we wish you, Dear Reader. Thanks for coming along for the first thirty years of Special Edition—we hope you'll be with us for many more!

We hope you enjoy *The Anniversary Party.*

Here's to the next thirty!

All the best,

Gail Chasan
Senior Editor, Special Edition

Chapter One
by RaeAnne Thayne

With the basket of crusty bread sticks she had baked that afternoon in one arm and a mixed salad—*insalata mista,* as the Italians would say—in the other, Melissa Morgan walked into her sister's house and her jaw dropped.

"Oh, my word, Ab! This looks incredible! When did you start decorating? A month ago?"

Predictably, Abby looked a little wild-eyed. Her sister was one of those type A personalities who always sought perfection, whether that was excelling in her college studies, where she'd emerged with a summa cum laude, or decorating for their parents' surprise thirtieth anniversary celebration.

Abby didn't answer for a moment. She was busy

arranging a plant in the basket of a rusty bicycle resting against one wall so the greenery spilled over the top, almost to the front tire. Melissa had no idea how she'd managed it but somehow Abby had hung wooden lattice from her ceiling to form a faux pergola over her dining table. Grapevines, fairy lights and more greenery had been woven through the lattice and, at various intervals, candles hung in colored jars like something out of a Tuscan vineyard.

Adorning the walls were framed posters of Venice and the beautiful and calming Lake Como.

"It feels like a month," Abby finally answered, "but actually, I only started last week. Greg helped me hang the lattice. I couldn't have done it without him."

The affection in her sister's voice caused a funny little twinge inside Melissa. Abby and her husband had one of those perfect relationships. They clearly adored each other, no matter what.

She wished she could say the same thing about Josh. After a year of dating, shouldn't she have a little more confidence in their relationship? If someone had asked her a month ago if she thought her boyfriend loved her, she would have been able to answer with complete assurance in the affirmative, but for the past few weeks something had changed. He'd been acting so oddly—dodging phone calls, canceling plans, avoiding her questions.

He seemed to be slipping away more every day. As melodramatic as it sounded, she didn't know how she would survive if he decided to break things off.

Breathe, she reminded herself. She didn't want to ruin the anniversary dinner by worrying about Josh. For now, she really needed to focus on her wonderful parents and how very much they deserved this celebration she and Abby had been planning for a long time.

"You and Greg have really outdone yourself. I love all the little details. The old wine bottles, the flowers. Just beautiful. I know Mom and Dad will be thrilled with your hard work." She paused. "I can only see one little problem."

Abby looked vaguely panicked. "What? What's missing?"

Melissa shook her head ruefully. "Nothing. That's the problem. I was supposed to be helping you. That's why I'm here early, right? Have you left anything for me to do?"

"Are you kidding? I've still got a million things to do. The chicken cacciatore is just about ready to go into the oven. Why don't you help me set the table?"

"Sure," she said, following her sister into the kitchen.

"You talked to Louise, right?" Abby asked.

"Yes. She had everything ready when I stopped at her office on my way over here. I've got a huge gift basket in the car. You should see it. She really went all out. Biscotti, gourmet cappuccino mix, even a bottle of prosecco."

"What about the tickets and the itinerary?" Abby had that panicked look again.

"Relax, Abs. It's all there. She's been amazing. I think she just might be as scarily organized as you are."

Abby made a face. "Did you have a chance to go over the details?"

"She printed everything out and included a copy for us, as well as Mom and Dad. In addition to the plane tickets and the hotel information and the other goodies, she sent over pamphlets, maps, even an Italian-English dictionary and a couple of guide-books."

"Perfect! They're going to be so surprised."

"Surprised and happy, I hope," Melissa answered, loading her arms with the deep red chargers and honey-gold plates her sister indicated, which perfectly matched the theme for the evening.

"How could they be anything else? They finally have the chance to enjoy the perfect honeymoon they missed out on the first time." Abby smiled, looking more than a little starry-eyed. Despite being married for several years, her sister was a true romantic.

"This has to be better than the original," she said. "The bar was set pretty low thirty years ago, judging by all the stories they've told us over the years. Missed trains, lousy hotels, disappearing luggage."

"Don't forget the pickpocket that stole their cash and passports."

Melissa had to smile. Though their parents'

stories always made their honeymoon thirty years ago sound dismal, Frank and Diane always laughed when they shared them, as if they had viewed the whole thing as a huge adventure.

She wanted that. She wanted to share that kind of joy and laughter and tears with Josh. The adventure that was life.

Her smile faded, replaced by that ache of sadness that always seemed so close these days. *Oh, Josh.* She reached into the silverware drawer, avoiding her sister's gaze.

"Okay. What's wrong?" Abby asked anyway.

She forced a smile. "Nothing. I'm just a little tired, that's all."

"Late night with Josh?" her sister teased.

Before she could stop them, tears welled up and spilled over. She blinked them back but not before her sharp-eyed sister caught them.

"What did I say?" Abby asked with a stunned look.

"Nothing. I just…I didn't have a late night with Josh. Not last night, not last week, not for the last two weeks. He's avoiding my calls and canceled our last two dates. Even when we're together, it's like he's not there. I know he's busy at work but…I think he's planning to break up with me."

Abby's jaw sagged and Melissa saw shock and something else, something furtive, shift across Abby's expression.

"That can't be true. It just…can't be."

She wanted to believe that, too. "I'm sorry. I

shouldn't have said anything. Forget it. You've worked so hard to make this night perfect and I don't want to ruin it."

Abby shook her head. "You need to put that wacky idea out of your head right now. Josh is crazy about you. It's clear to anybody who has ever seen the two of you together for five seconds. He couldn't possibly be thinking of breaking things off."

"I'm sure you're right," she lied. Too much evidence pointed otherwise. Worst of all was the casual kiss good-night the past few times she'd seen him, instead of one of their deep, emotional, soul-sharing kisses that made her toes curl.

"I'm serious, Missy. Trust me on this. I'm absolutely positive he's not planning to break up with you. Not Josh. He loves you. In fact…"

She stopped, biting her lip, and furiously turned back to the chicken.

"In fact what?"

Abby's features were evasive. "In fact, would he be out right now with Greg buying the wine and champagne for tonight if he didn't want to have anything to do with the Morgan family?"

Out of the corner of her gaze, Melissa saw that amazingly decorated dining room again, the magical setting her sister had worked so hard to create for their parents who loved each other dearly. She refused to ruin this night for Abby and the rest of her family. For now, she would focus on the celebration and forget the tiny cracks in her heart.

She pasted on a smile and grabbed the napkins,

with their rings formed out of entwined grapevine hearts. "You're right. I'm being silly. I'm sure everything will be just fine. Anyway, tonight is for Mom and Dad. That's the important thing."

Abby gave her a searching look and Melissa couldn't help thinking that even with the worry lines on her forehead, Abby seemed to glow tonight.

"It is about them, isn't it?" Abby murmured. Though Melissa's arms were full, her sister reached around the plates and cutlery to give her a hug. "Trust me, baby sister. Everything will be just fine."

Melissa dearly wanted to believe her and as she returned to the dining room, she did her very best to ignore the ache of fear that something infinitely dear was slipping away.

"Hello? Are you still in there?"

His friend Greg's words jerked Josh out of his daze and he glanced up. "Yeah. Sorry. Did you say something?"

"Only about three times. I've been asking your opinion about the champagne and all I'm getting in return is a blank stare. You're a million miles away, man, which is not really helping out much here."

This just might be the most important day of his life. Who could blame a guy if he couldn't seem to string two thoughts together?

"Sorry. I've got a lot of things on my mind."

"And champagne is obviously not one of those things."

He made a face. "It rarely is. I'm afraid I'm more of a Sam Adams kind of guy."

"I hear you. Why do you think I asked you to come along and help me pick out the wine and champagne for tonight?"

He had wondered that himself. "Because my car has a bigger trunk?"

Greg laughed, which eased Josh's nerves a little. He had to admit, he had liked the guy since he met him a year ago when he first started dating Melissa. Josh was married to Melissa's sister, Abby, and if things worked out the way he hoped, they would be brothers-in-law in the not-so-distant future.

"It's only the six of us for dinner," Greg reminded him. "I'm not exactly buying cases here. So what do you think?"

He turned back to the racks of bottles. "No idea. Which one is more expensive?"

Greg picked one up with a fancy label that certainly looked pricey.

"Excellent choice." The snooty clerk who had mostly been ignoring them since they walked in finally deigned to approach them.

"You think so?" Greg asked. "We're celebrating a big occasion."

"You won't be disappointed, I assure you. What else can I help you find?"

Sometime later—and with considerably lightened wallets—the two of them carried two magnums of champagne and two bottles of wine out to Josh's car.

"I, uh, need to make one last quick stop," he said after pulling into traffic. "Do you mind waiting?"

"No problem. The party doesn't start for another two hours. We've got plenty of time."

When Josh pulled up in front of an assuming storefront a few moments later, Greg looked at the sign above the door then back at him with eyebrows raised. "Wow. Seriously? Tonight? I thought Abby was jumping the gun when she said she suspected you were close to proposing. She's always right, that beautiful wife of mine. Don't tell her I said that."

Josh shifted, uncomfortably aware his fingers were shaking a little as he undid his seatbelt. "I bought the ring two weeks ago. When the jeweler told me it would be ready today, I figured that was a sign."

"You're a brave man to pick a ring out without her."

Panic clutched at his gut again, but he took a deep breath and pushed it away. He wanted to make his proposal perfect. Part of that, to his mind, was the element of surprise.

"I found a bridal magazine at Melissa's apartment kind of hidden under a stack of books and she had the page folded down on this ring. I snapped a quick picture with my phone and took that in to the jeweler."

"Nice." Greg's admiring look settled his stomach a little.

"I figure, if she doesn't like it, we can always reset the stone, right?"

"So when are you going to pop the question?"

"I haven't figured that out yet. I thought maybe when I take her home after the party tonight, we might drive up to that overlook above town."

"That could work."

"What about you? How did you propose to Abby?"

"Nothing very original, I'm afraid. I took her to dinner at La Maison Marie. She loves that place. Personally, I think you're only paying for overpriced sauce, but what can you do? Anyway, after dinner, she kept acting like she was expecting something. I *did* take her along to shop for rings a few weeks earlier but hadn't said anything to her since. She seemed kind of disappointed when the dessert came and no big proposal. So we were walking around on the grounds after dinner and we walked past this waterfall and pond she liked. I pretended I tripped over something and did a stupid little magician sleight of hand and pulled out the ring box."

"Did you do the whole drop-to-your-knee thing?"

"Yeah. It seemed important to Abby. Women remember that kind of thing."

"I hope I don't forget that part."

"Don't sweat it. When the moment comes, whatever you do will be right for the two of you, I promise."

"I hope so."

The depth of his love for Melissa still took him by surprise. He loved her with everything inside him and wanted to give her all the hearts and flowers and romance she could ever want.

"It will be," Greg said. "Anyway, look at how lousy Frank and Diane's marriage started out. Their honeymoon sounded like a nightmare but thirty years later they can still laugh about it."

That was what he wanted with Melissa. Thirty years—and more—of laughter and joy and love.

He just had to get through the proposal first.

Chapter Two
by Christine Rimmer

"Frank. The light is yellow. Frank!" Diana Morgan stomped the passenger-side floor of the Buick. Hard. If only she had the brakes on her side.

Frank Morgan pulled to a smooth stop as the light went red. "There," he said, in that calm, deep, untroubled voice she'd always loved. "We're stopped. No need to wear a hole in the floor."

Diana glanced over at her husband of thirty years. She loved him so much. There were a whole lot of things to worry about in life, but Frank's love was the one thing Diana never doubted. He belonged to her, absolutely, as she belonged to him, and he'd given her two beautiful, perfect daughters. Abby and Melissa were all grown up now.

The years went by way too fast.

Diana sent her husband another glance. Thirty years together. Amazing. She still loved just looking at him. He was the handsomest man she'd ever met, even at fifty-seven. Nature had been kind to him. He had all his hair and it was only lightly speckled with gray. She smoothed her own shoulder-length bob. No gray there, either. Her hair was still the same auburn shade it had been when she married him. Only in her case, nature didn't have a thing to do with it.

A man only grew more distinguished over the years. A woman had to work at it.

The light turned green. Frank hit the gas.

Too hard, Diana thought. But she didn't say a word. She only straightened her teal-blue silk blouse, re-crossed her legs and tried not to make impatient, worried noises. Frank was a wonderful man. But he drove too fast.

Abby and her husband, Greg, were having them over for dinner tonight. They were on their way there now—to Abby's house. Diana was looking forward to the evening. But she was also dreading it. Something was going on with Abby. A mother knows these things.

And something was bothering Melissa, too. Diana's younger daughter was still single. She'd been going out with Josh Wright for a year now. It was a serious relationship.

But was there something wrong between Josh and Melissa? Diana had a sense about these things, a sort of radar for emotional disturbances, especially when it came to her daughters. Right now, tonight, Diana had a suspicion that something wasn't right—both between Melissa and Josh *and* between Abby and Greg.

"Remember Venice?" Frank gave her a fond glance.

She smiled at him—and then stiffened. "Frank. Eyes on the road."

"All right, all right." He patiently faced front again. "Remember that wonderful old hotel on the Grand Canal?"

She made a humphing sound. "It was like the rest of our honeymoon. Nothing went right."

"I loved every moment of it," he said softly.

She reminded him, "You know what happened at that hotel in Venice, how they managed to lose our luggage somewhere between the front desk and our room. How hard can it be, to get the suitcases to the right room? And it smelled a bit moldy in the bathroom, didn't you think?"

"All I remember is you, Diana. Naked in the morning light." He said it softly. Intimately.

She shivered a little, drew in a shaky breath and confessed, "Oh, yes. That. I remember that, too." It was one of the best things about a good marriage. The shared memories. Frank had seen her naked in Venice when they were both young. Together, they had heard Abby's first laugh, watched Melissa as she learned to walk, staggering and falling, but then gamely picking herself right back up and trying again. Together, they had made it through all those years that drew them closer, through the rough times as well as the happy ones....

A good marriage.

Until very recently, she'd been so sure that Abby and Greg were happy. But were they? Really? And what about Melissa and Josh?

Oh, Lord. Being a mother was the hardest job in the world. They grew up. But they stayed in your heart. And when they were suffering, you ached right along with them.

"All right," Frank said suddenly in an exasperated tone. "You'd better just tell me, Diana. You'd better just say it, whatever it is."

Diana sighed. Deeply. "Oh, Frank..."

"Come on," he coaxed, pulling to another stop at yet another stoplight—at the very last possible second. She didn't even stomp the floor that time, she was that upset. "Tell me," he insisted.

Tears pooled in her eyes and clogged her throat. She sniffed them back. "I wasn't going to do it. I wasn't going to interfere. I wasn't even going to say a word..."

He flipped open the armrest and whipped out a tissue. "Dry your eyes."

"Oh, Frank..." She took the tissue and dabbed at her lower lid. If she wasn't careful, her makeup would be a total mess.

"Now," Frank said, reaching across to pat her knee. "Tell me about it. Whatever it is, you know you'll feel better once we've talked it over."

The light changed. "Go," she said on a sob.

He drove on. "I'm waiting."

She sniffed again. "I think something's wrong between Abby and Greg. And not only that, there's something going on with Melissa, too. I think Melissa's got…a secret, you know? A secret that is worrying her terribly."

"Why do you think something's going on between Abby and Greg?"

"I sensed it. You know how sensitive I am— Oh, God. Do you think Abby and Greg are breaking up? Do you think he might be seeing someone else?"

"Whoa. Diana. Slow down."

"Well, I am *worried.* I am *so* worried. And Melissa. She is suffering. I can hear it in her voice when I talk to her."

"But you haven't told me *why* you think there might be something wrong—with Melissa, or between Abby and Greg. Did Abby say something to you?"

"Of course not. She wants to protect me."

"What about Melissa?"

"What do you *mean,* what about Melissa?"

"Well, did you *ask* her if something is bothering her?"

Another sob caught in Diana's throat. She swallowed it. "I couldn't. I didn't want to butt in."

Frank eased the car to the shoulder and stopped. "Diana," he said. That was all. Just her name.

It was more than enough. "Don't you look at me like that, Frank Morgan."

"Diana, I hate to say this—"

"Then don't. Just don't. And why are we stopped? We'll be late. Even with family, you know I always like to be on time."

"Diana…"

She waved her soggy tissue at him. "Drive, Frank. Just drive."

He leaned closer across the console. "Sweetheart…"

She sagged in her seat. "Oh, fine. What?"

"You know what you're doing, don't you?" He said it gently. But still. She knew exactly what he was getting at and she didn't like it one bit.

She sighed and dropped the wadded tissue in the little wastepaper bag she always carried in the car. "Well, I know you're bound to tell me, now don't I?"

He took her hand, kissed the back of it.

"Don't try to butter me up," she muttered.

"You're jumping to conclusions again," he said tenderly.

"Am not."

"Yes, you are. You've got nothin'. Zip. Admit it. No solid reason why you think Melissa has a secret or why you think Abby and Greg are suddenly on the rocks."

"I don't need a solid reason. I can *feel* it." She laid her hand over her heart. "Here."

"You know it's very possible that what's really going on is a surprise anniversary party for us, don't you?"

Diana smoothed her hair. "What? You mean tonight?"

"That's right. Tonight."

"Oh, I suppose. It could be." She pictured their dear faces. She loved them so much. "They are the sweetest girls, aren't they?"

"The best. I'm the luckiest dad in the world—not to mention the happiest husband."

Diana leaned toward him and kissed him. "You *are* a very special man." She sank back against her seat—and remembered how worried she was. "But Frank, if this *is* a party, it's still not *it*."

"It?" He looked bewildered. Men could be so thickheaded sometimes.

Patiently, she reminded him, "The awful, secret things that are going on with our daughters."

He bent in close, kissed her cheek and then brushed his lips across her own. "We are going to dinner at our daughter's house," he whispered. "We are going to have a wonderful time. You are not going to snoop around trying to find out if something's wrong with Abby. You're not going to worry about Melissa."

"I hate you, Frank."

"No, you don't. You love me *almost* as much as I love you."

She wrinkled her nose at him. "More. I love you more."

He kissed her again. "Promise you won't snoop and you'll stop jumping to conclusions?"

"And if I don't, what? We'll sit here on the side of the road all night?"

"Promise."

"Fine. All right. I promise."

He touched her cheek, a lovely, cherishing touch. "Can we go to Abby's now?"

"I'm not the one who stopped the car."

He only looked at her reproachfully.

She couldn't hold out against him. She never could. "Oh, all right. I've promised, already, okay? Now, let's go."

With a wry smile, he retreated back behind the wheel and eased the car forward into the flow of traffic again.

Abby opened the door. "Surprise!" Abby, Greg, Melissa and Josh all shouted at once. They all started clapping.

Greg announced, "Happy Anniversary!" The rest of them chimed in with "Congratulations!" and "Thirty years!" and "Wahoo!"

Frank was laughing. "Well, what do you know?"

Diana said nothing. One look in her older daughter's big brown eyes and she knew for certain that she wasn't just imagining things. Something was going on in Abby's life. Something important.

They all filed into the dining room, where the walls were decorated with posters of the Grand Canal and the Tuscan countryside, of the Coliseum and the small, beautiful town of Bellagio on Lake

Como. The table was set with Abby's best china and tall candles gave a golden glow.

Greg said, "We thought, you know, an Italian theme—in honor of your honeymoon."

"It's lovely," said Diana, going through the motions, hugging first Greg and then Josh.

"Thank you," said Frank as he clapped his son-in-law on the back and shook hands with Josh.

Melissa came close. "Mom." She put on a smile. But her eyes were as shadowed as Abby's. "Happy thirtieth anniversary."

Diana grabbed her and hugged her. No doubt about it. Melissa looked miserable, too.

Yes, Diana had promised Frank that she would mind her own business.

But, well, sometimes a woman just couldn't keep that kind of promise. Sometimes a woman had to find a way to get to the bottom of a bad situation for the sake of the ones she loved most of all.

By the end of the evening, no matter what, Diana would find out the secrets her daughters were keeping from her.

Frank leaned close. "Don't even think about it."

She gave him her sweetest smile. "Happy anniversary, darling."

Chapter Three
by Susan Crosby

Abby Morgan DeSena and her husband, Greg, had hosted quite a few dinner parties during their three years of marriage, but none as special as this one—a celebration of Abby's parents' thirtieth wedding anniversary. Abby and her younger sister, Melissa, had spent weeks planning the Italian-themed party as a sweet reminder for their parents of their honeymoon, and now that the main meal was over, Abby could say, well, so far, so good.

For someone who planned everything down to the last detail, that was high praise. They were on schedule. First, antipasti and wine in the living room, then chicken cacciatore, crusty bread sticks and green salad in the dining room.

But for all that the timetable had been met and the food praised and devoured, an air of tension hovered over the six people at the table, especially between Melissa and her boyfriend, Josh, who were both acting out of character.

"We had chicken cacciatore our first night in Bellagio, remember, Diana?" Abby's father said to her mother as everyone sat back, sated. "And lemon sorbet in prosecco."

"The waiter knocked my glass into my lap," Diana reminded him.

"Your napkin caught most of it, and he fixed you another one. He even took it off the tab. On our newlywed budget, it made a difference." He brought his wife's hand to his lips, his eyes twinkling. "And it was delicious, wasn't it? Tart and sweet and bubbly."

Diana blushed, making Abby wonder if the memory involved more than food. It was inspiring seeing her parents so openly in love after thirty years.

Under the table, Abby felt her hand being squeezed and looked at her own beloved husband. Greg winked, as if reading her mind.

"Well, we don't have sorbet and prosecco," Abby said, standing and stacking dinner plates. "But we certainly have dessert. Please sit down, Mom. You're our guest. Melissa and I will take care of everything."

It didn't take long to clear the table.

"Mom and Dad loved the dinner, didn't they?"

Melissa asked as they entered Abby's contemporary kitchen.

"They seemed to," Abby answered, although unsure whether she believed her own words. Had her parents noticed the same tension Abby had? Her mother's gaze had flitted from Melissa to Josh to Abby to Greg all evening, as if searching for clues. It'd made Abby more nervous with every passing minute, and on a night she'd been looking forward to, a night of sweet surprises.

"How about you? Did you enjoy the meal?" Abby asked Melissa, setting dishes in the sink, then started the coffeemaker brewing. "You hardly touched your food."

She shrugged. "I guess I snacked on too many bread sticks before dinner."

Abby took out a raspberry tiramisu from the refrigerator while studying her sister, noting how stiffly Melissa held herself, how shaky her hands were as she rinsed the dinner plates. She seemed fragile. It wasn't a word Abby usually applied to her sister. The conversation they'd had earlier in the evening obviously hadn't set Melissa's mind at ease, but Abby didn't know what else to say to her tightly wrung sister. Only time—and Josh—could relieve Melissa's anxiety.

Abby set the fancy dessert on the counter next to six etched-crystal parfait glasses.

Melissa approached, drying her hands, then picked up one of the glasses. "Grandma gave these to you, didn't she?"

"Mmm-hmm. Three years ago as a wedding present. I know it's a cliché, but it seems like yesterday." Abby smiled at her sister, remembering the wedding, revisiting her wonderful marriage. She couldn't ask for a better husband, friend and partner than Greg. "Grandma plans to give you the other six glasses at your wedding. When we both have big family dinners, we can share them. It'll be our tradition."

Melissa's face paled. Her eyes welled. Horrified, Abby dropped the spoon and reached for her.

"I—I'll grab the gift basket from your office," Melissa said, taking a couple steps back then rushing out.

Frustrated, Abby pressed her face into her hands. If she were the screaming type, she would've screamed. If she were a throw-the-pots-around type, she would've done that, too, as noisily as possible. It would've felt *good*.

"I thought Melissa was in here with you," said a male voice from behind her.

Abby spun around and glared at Josh Wright, the source of Melissa's problems—and subsequently Abby's—as he peeked into the kitchen. He could be the solution, too, if only he'd act instead of sitting on his hands.

"She's getting the anniversary gift from my office," Abby said through gritted teeth, digging deep for the composure she'd inherited from her father.

Josh came all the way into the room. He looked

as strained as Melissa. "Need some help?" he asked, shoving his hands into his pockets instead of going in search of Melissa.

"Coward." Abby began dishing up six portions of tiramisu.

"Guilty," Josh said, coming up beside her. "Give me a job. I can't sit still."

"You can pour the decaf into that carafe next to the coffeemaker."

Full of nervous energy, his hands shaking as much as Melissa's had earlier, he got right to the task, fumbling at every step, slopping coffee onto the counter.

"Relax, would you, Josh?" Abby said, exasperated. "You're making everyone jumpy, but especially Melissa. My sister is her mother's daughter, you know. They both have a flair for the dramatic, but this time Melissa is honestly thrown by your behavior. She's on the edge, and it's not of her own making."

"But it'll all come out okay in the end?"

The way he turned the sentence into a question had Abby staring at him. He and her kid sister were a study in contrasts, Melissa with her black hair and green eyes, Josh all blond and blue-eyed. They'd been dating for a year, were head over heels in love with each other, seeming to validate the theory that opposites attract. It was rare that they weren't touching or staring into each other's eyes, communicating silently.

Tonight was different, however, and Abby knew

why. She just didn't know if they would all survive the suspense.

"Whether or not it all turns out okay in the end depends on how long you take to pop the question," Abby said, dropping her voice to a whisper.

"You know I'm planning the perfect proposal," he whispered back. "Your husband gave me advice, but if you'd like to add yours, I'm listening."

She couldn't tell him that Melissa thought he was about to break up with her—that was hers to say. But Abby could offer some perspective.

"Here's my advice, Josh, and it has nothing to do with how to set a romantic scene that she'll remember the rest of her life. My advice is simple—do it sooner rather than later." She spoke in a normal tone again, figuring even if someone came into the room, they wouldn't suspect what she and Josh were talking about. "When Greg and I were in college, I misunderstood something he said. Instead of asking him to clarify it, I stewed. And stewed some more. I blew it all out of proportion."

She dug deep into memories she'd long ago put aside. "Here's what happens to a couple at times like that. He asks what's wrong, and she says it's nothing. He asks again. She *insists* it's nothing. A gulf widens that can't be crossed because there's no longer a bridge between them, one you used to travel easily. It doesn't even matter how much love you share. Once trust is gone, once the ability to talk to each other openly and freely goes away, the relationship begins to unravel. Sometimes it takes weeks, sometimes months, even years, but it happens and there's no fixing it."

"But you fixed it."

They almost hadn't, Abby remembered. They came so close to breaking up. "At times like that, it can go either way. Even strong partners struggle sometimes in a marriage."

"How do you get through those times?"

"You put on a smile for everyone, then you try to work it out alone together so that no one else gets involved."

"Don't you talk to your mom? She's had a long, successful marriage. She'd give good advice, wouldn't she?"

Abby smiled as she pictured her sweet, sometimes overwrought mother. "Mom's the last one I'd ask for advice," she said.

"I'm going to see what's taking so long," Diana said to her husband, laying her napkin on the table.

"Diana." Implied in his tone of voice were the words he didn't speak aloud—*Don't borrow trouble.*

"I'm sure they'll be right out," Greg said, standing, suddenly looking frantic. Her cool, calm son-in-law never panicked.

It upped her determination to see what was wrong. Because something definitely was.

"I'm going." Diana headed toward the kitchen. She could hear Abby speaking quietly.

"I adore my mother, but she makes mountains out of molehills. Greg and I are a team. We keep our problems to ourselves. And you know she would take my side, as any parent would, and that isn't fair to Greg. She might hold on to her partiality long after I've forgotten the argument. So you see, Josh, sometimes the best way to handle personal problems is to keep other people in the dark. Got it?"

"Clear as a bell."

Diana slapped a hand over her mouth and slid a few feet along the wall outside the kitchen before she let out an audible gasp. Her first born *was* keeping her in the dark about something, just as Diana had suspected. And Frank had pooh-poohed the whole thing.

Men just didn't get it. It wasn't called women's intuition for nothing—and she wasn't just a woman but a mother. Mothers saw every emotion on their children's faces, knew every body movement.

She'd *known* something was wrong with Abby. Now it'd been verified, not by rumor but by the person in question, no less. Abby and Greg were on the verge of separating. Her daughter had hidden their problems, not seeking advice from the one who loved her most in the world. Diana could've helped, too, she was sure of it.

Keep other people in the dark. The words stung. She wasn't "other people." She was Abby's mother.

And what about Melissa? What was her problem—because she definitely had one, something big, too. Had she confided in Abby?

Diana moved out of range, not wanting to hear more distressing words, not on the anniversary of the most wonderful day of her life. But she had to tell Frank what she'd learned, had to share the awful news with her own partner so that she could make it through the rest of the evening.

At least she could count on Frank to understand.

She hoped.

Chapter Four
by Christyne Butler

Don't think, don't feel.

Just keep breathing and you'll get through this night unscathed.

Unscathed, but with a broken heart.

Melissa squared her shoulders, brushed the wetness from her cheeks and heaved a shuddering breath that shook her all the way to her toes.

There. Don't you feel calmer?

No, she didn't, but that wasn't anyone's fault but her own.

She'd fallen in love with Josh on their very first date and after tonight, she'd probably never see him again.

The past two weeks had been crazy at her job.

Trying to make it through what had been ten hours without her usual caffeine fix, having decided that two cups of coffee and three diet sodas a day weren't the best thing for her, had taken its toll. She'd been moody and pissy and okay, she was big to admit it, a bit dramatic.

Hey, she was her mother's daughter.

But none of that explained why the man of her dreams was going to break her heart.

Another deep breath did little to help, but it would have to do. Between helping her sister plan tonight's party and Josh's strange behavior, Melissa knew she was holding herself together with the thinnest of threads.

The scent of fresh coffee drifted through the house and Melissa groaned. Oh, how she ached for a hot cup, swimming in cream and lots of sugar.

Pushing the thought from her head, she picked up the gift basket that held everything her parents would need for a perfect second honeymoon in Italy. There was a small alcove right next to the dining room, a perfect place to stash it until just the right moment.

Turning, she headed for the door of her sister's office when the matching antique photo frames on a nearby bookshelf caught her eye.

The one on the right, taken just a few short years ago, was of Abby and Greg standing at the altar just after being presented to their friends and family as Mr. and Mrs. Gregory DeSena. Despite the elaborate setting, and the huge bridal party standing other either side of them, Melissa right there next to her sister, Abby and Greg only had eyes for each other. In fact, the photographer had captured the picture just as Greg had gently wiped a tear from her sister's cheek.

The other photograph, a bit more formal in monochrome colors of black and white, showed her mother and father on their wedding day. Her mother looked so young, so beautiful, so thin. Daddy was as handsome as ever in his tuxedo, his arm around his bride, his hand easily spanning her waist. The bridal bouquet was larger and over-the-top, typical for the early 80's, but her mother's dress...

Melissa squeezed tighter to the basket, the cellophane crinkling loudly in the silent room.

Abby had planned her wedding with the precision of an army general, right down to her chiffon, A-line silhouette gown with just enough crystal bling along the shoulder straps to give a special sparkle. Their mother looked the opposite, but just as beautiful wearing her own mother's gown, a vintage 1960 beauty of satin, lace and tulle with a circular skirt that cried out for layers of crinoline, a square-neck bodice and sleeves that hugged her arms.

A dress that Melissa had always seen herself wearing one day.

The day she married Josh.

Of course, she'd change into something short and sexy and perfect for dancing the night away after the ceremony, but—

"Oh, what does it matter!" Melissa said aloud. "It's not going to happen! It's never going to happen. Josh doesn't want to date you anymore, much less even think about getting down on one knee."

She exited the room and hurried down the long hall, tucking the basket just out of sight. They would have dessert, present the gift and then she would find a way to get Josh to take her home as soon as possible.

For the last time.

This was all Greg's fault.

As heartbreaking as it was, because she and Frank had always loved Greg, Diana knew deep in her heart that the man they'd welcomed in their home, into their hearts, was on the verge of walking out on their daughter.

How could Greg do this to Abby?

They were perfect together, complemented each other so well because they were so alike. Level-headed, organized to a fault, methodical even.

Diana paused and grabbed hold of the stairway landing.

Could that be it?

Could Abby and Greg be too much alike? Had her son-in-law found someone else? Someone cute and bubbly who hung on his every word like it was gold?

Abby had mentioned a coworker of Greg's they'd run into one night while out to dinner. She'd said he'd been reluctant to introduce them, which seemed strange as the woman had literally gushed at how much she enjoyed working with Abby's husband when she'd stopped by their table.

The need to get to Frank, to squeeze his hand and have him comfort her, rolled over Diana. She needed him to tell her that everything would be all right, that she'd been right all along, and promise her they'd fight tooth and nail for their daughter so she didn't lose this beautiful home.

"Mom?"

Diana looked up and found Melissa standing there.

"Are you okay?" Melissa asked. "You look a little pale."

"I'm fine."

"You've got a death grip on the railing."

Diana immediately released her hold. "I just got a bit light-headed for a moment."

Concern filled her daughter's beautiful eyes. She motioned to the steps that led to the second floor. "Here, let's sit."

"But your sister is—"

"Perfectly capable of pulling dessert together all on her own," Melissa took her arm and the two of them sat. "Disgustingly capable, as we both know."

Diana sat, basically because she had no choice, taking the time to really look at her daughter. She'd been crying. Her baby suffered the same fate as she did when tears came—puffy eyes. And while Melissa had been acting strange during dinner, this was the first true evidence Diana had that something was terribly wrong.

"Darling, you seem a bit...off this evening." Diana kept her tone light after a few minutes of silence passed. "How is everything with you? You didn't eat very much tonight."

Melissa stared at her clenched hands. "Everything is just fine, mother. It's been a long week and I'm very tired."

"Yes, you said you've been working long hours. That's probably cut into your free time with Josh."

"Y-yes, it has, but I don't think that's going to be a problem much longer."

"What does that mean?"

Melissa rose, one hand pressed against her stomach. "It's nothing. You were right. We should get back into the dining room. You know how Abby gets when things go off schedule."

Yes, she did know. Oh, the divorce was going to upset Abby's tidy world, but that didn't mean that Diana wouldn't be there for her other daughter, as well. She still had no idea what was bothering her youngest, but she would find out before this evening was through.

And she would make things right.

For both her girls.

She'd easily found the time to attend Abby's debates, girl scout meetings and band concerts and never missed a dance recital, theatre production or football game while Melissa was on the cheerleading squad. Her daughters might be grown, but they still needed their mother.

Now more than ever.

Diana stood, as well. "Yes, let's go back and join everyone."

They walked into the room and Diana's gaze locked with Frank's. Her husband watched her every step as she moved around the table to retake her seat next to him. Thirty years of marriage honed his deduction skills to a razor-sharp point, and she knew that he knew she'd found out something.

"Okay, let's get this celebration going." Greg spoke from where he stood at the buffet filling tall fluted glasses with sparkling liquid, having already popped open the bottle. "Josh, why don't you hand out the champagne to everyone?"

Frank leaned in close. "What's wrong?"

Diana batted her eyes, determined not to cry as his gentle and caring tone was sure to bring on the waterworks. "Not now, darling."

"So you were worried for nothing?"

"Of course not. I was right all along—" She cut off her words when Abby came in with a tray of desserts in her hands. "Dear, can I help with those?"

"No, you stay seated, Mom. It'll only take me a moment to hand these out."

True to her words, the etched-crystal parfait dishes were soon at everyone's place setting and, immediately after, Josh placed a glass in front of Frank and Diana.

Diana watched as he then went back to get two

more for Greg and Abby and one last trip for the final two glasses.

"Here you go, sweetheart." He moved in behind Melissa and reached past her shoulder to place a glass in front of her.

"No, thank you." Her baby girl's voice was strained.

"You don't want any champagne?" Josh was clearly confused. "You love the stuff. We practically finished off a magnum ourselves last New Year's Eve."

Melissa shook her head, her dark locks flying over her shoulder. "I'm sure. I'll just h-have—" She paused, pressing her fingertips to her mouth for a quick moment. "I'd prefer a cup of coffee. Decaf, please."

Oh, everything made sense now!

The tears, the exhaustion, the hand held protectively over her still flat belly, the refusal of alcohol. Her motherly intrusion might have been late in picking up on Melissa's distress, but the realization over what her baby was facing hit Diana like a thunderbolt coming from the sky.

Her heart didn't know whether to break for the certain pain Abby was facing over the end of her marriage or rejoice with the news that she was finally going to be a grandmother!

Her baby was having a baby!

Chapter Five
by Gina Wilkins

During the year he and Melissa Morgan had been together, Josh Wright thought he'd come to know her family fairly well, but there were still times when he felt like an outsider who couldn't quite catch on to the family rhythms. Tonight was one of those occasions.

The undercurrents of tension at the elegantly set dinner table were obvious enough, even to him.

Melissa had been acting oddly all evening. Abby and Greg kept exchanging significant looks, as though messages passed between them that no one else could hear. Even Melissa and Abby's mom, Diana, typically the life of any dinner party, was unnaturally subdued and introspective tonight. Only the family patriarch, Frank, seemed as steady and unruffled as ever, characteristically enjoying the time with his family without getting drawn in to their occasional, usually Diana-generated melodramas.

Josh didn't have a clue what was going on with any of them. Shouldn't he understand them better by now, considering he wanted so badly to be truly one of them soon?

He dipped his spoon into the dessert dish in front of him, scooping up a bite of fresh raspberries, an orange-liqueur flavored mascarpone cheese mixture and ladyfingers spread with what tasted like raspberry jam. "Abby, this dessert is amazing."

She smiled across the table at him. "Thank you. Mom and Dad had tiramisu the first night of their honeymoon, so I tried to recreate that nice memory."

"Ours wasn't flavored with orange and raspberry," Diana seemed compelled to point out. "We had a more traditional espresso-based tiramisu."

Abby's smile turned just a bit wry. "I found this recipe online and thought it sounded good. I wasn't trying to exactly reproduce what you had before, Mom."

"I think this one is even better," Frank interjected hastily, after swallowing a big bite of his dessert. "Who'd have thought thirty years later we'd be eating tiramisu made by our own little girl, eh, Diana?"

Everyone smiled—except Melissa, who was

playing with her dessert without her usual enthusiasm for sweets. It bothered Josh that Melissa seemed to become more withdrawn and somber as the evening progressed. Though she had made a noticeable effort to participate in the dining table conversation, her eyes were darkened to almost jade and the few smiles she'd managed looked forced. As well as he knew her, as much as he loved her, he sensed when she was stressed or unhappy. For some reason, she seemed both tonight, and that was twisting him into knots.

Maybe Abby had been right when she'd warned him that his nervous anticipation was affecting Melissa, though he thought he'd done a better job of hiding it from her. Apparently, she knew him a bit too well, also.

Encouraged by the response to his compliment of the dessert, he thought he would try again to keep the conversation light and cheerful. Maybe Melissa would relax if everyone else did.

Mindful of the reason for this gathering—and because he was rather obsessed with love and marriage, anyway—he said, "Thirty years. That's a remarkable accomplishment these days. Not many couples are able to keep the fire alive for that long."

He couldn't imagine his passion for Melissa ever burning out, not in thirty years—or fifty, for that matter.

He felt her shift in her seat next to him and her spoon clicked against her dessert dish. He glanced sideways at her, but she was looking down at her dish, her glossy black hair falling forward to hide her face from him.

Frank, at least, seemed pleased with Josh's observation.

"That's it, exactly." Frank pointed his spoon in Josh's direction, almost dripping raspberry jam on the tablecloth. "Keeping the fire alive. Takes work, but it's worth it, right, hon?"

"Absolutely." Diana looked hard at Abby and Greg as she spoke. "All marriages go through challenging times, but with love and patience and mutual effort, the rewards will come."

Abby and Greg shared a startled look, but Frank spoke again before either of them could respond to what seemed like a sermon aimed directly at them. "I still remember the day I met her, just like it was yesterday."

That sounded like a story worth pursuing. Though everyone else had probably heard it many times, Josh encouraged Frank to continue. "I'd like to hear about it. How did you meet?"

Frank's smile was nostalgic, his eyes distant with the memories. "I was the best man in a college friend's wedding. Diana was the maid of honor. I had a flat tire on the way to the wedding rehearsal, so I was late arriving."

Diana shook her head. Though she still looked worried about something, she was paying attention to her husband's tale. "The bride was fit to be tied that it looked as though the best man wasn't going to show up for the rehearsal. She was a nervous wreck, even though her groom kept assuring her Frank could be counted on to be there."

Frank chuckled. "Anyway, the minute I arrived, all rumpled and dusty from changing the tire, I was rushed straight to a little room off the church sanctuary where the groom's party was gathered getting ready to enter on cue. I didn't have a chance to socialize or meet the other wedding party members before the rehearsal began. Five minutes after I dashed in, I was standing at the front of the church next to my friend Jim. And then the music began and the bridesmaids started their march in. Diana was the third bridesmaid to enter."

"Gretchen was first, Bridget next."

Ignoring the details Diana inserted, Frank continued, "She was wearing a green dress, the same color as her eyes. The minute she walked into the church, I felt my heart flop like a landed fish."

Diana laughed ruefully. "Well, that doesn't sound very romantic."

Frank patted her hand, still lost in his memories. "She stopped halfway down the aisle and informed the organist that she was playing much too slowly and that everyone in the audience would fall asleep before the whole wedding party reached the front of the church."

"Well, she was."

Frank chuckled and winked at Josh. "That was when I knew this was someone I had to meet."

Charmed by the story, Josh remembered the first moment he'd laid eyes on Melissa. He understood that "floppy fish" analogy all too well, though he'd compared his own heart to a runaway train. He could still recall how hard it had raced when Melissa had tossed back her dark hair and laughed up at him for the first time, her green eyes sparkling with humor and warmth. He'd actually wondered for a moment if she could hear it pounding against his chest.

"So it was love at first sight?"

Frank nodded decisively. "That it was."

"And when did you know she was 'the one' for you? That you wanted to marry her?"

"Probably right then. But certainly the next evening during the ceremony, after I'd spent a few hours getting to know Diana. When I found myself mentally saying 'I do' when the preacher asked 'Do you take this woman?' I knew I was hooked."

Josh sighed. This, he thought, was why he wanted to wait for the absolute perfect moment to propose to Melissa. Someday he hoped to tell a story that would make everyone who heard it say "Awww," the way he felt like doing now. "You're a lucky man, Frank. Not every guy is fortunate enough to find a woman he wants to spend the rest of his life with."

Three lucky men sat at this table tonight, he thought happily. Like Frank and Greg, he had found his perfect match.

Melissa dropped her spoon with a clatter and sprang to her feet. "I, uh— Excuse me," she muttered, her voice choked. "I'm not feeling well."

Before Josh or anyone else could ask her what

was wrong, she dashed from the room. Concerned, he half rose from his seat, intending to follow her.

"What on earth is wrong with Melissa?" Frank asked in bewilderment.

Words burst from Diana as if she'd held them in as long as she was physically able. "Melissa is pregnant."

His knees turning to gelatin, Josh fell back into his chair with a thump.

After patting her face with a towel, Melissa looked in the bathroom mirror to make sure she'd removed all signs of her bout of tears. She was quite sure Abby would say she was overreacting and being overly dramatic—just like their Mom, Abby would say with a shake of her auburn head—but Melissa couldn't help it. Every time she thought about her life without Josh in it tears welled up behind her eyes and it was all she could do to keep them from gushing out.

Abby had tried to convince her she was only imagining that Josh was trying to find a way to break up with her. As much as she wanted to believe her sister, Melissa was convinced her qualms were well-founded. She knew every expression that crossed Josh's handsome face. Every flicker of emotion that passed through his clear blue eyes. He had grown increasingly nervous and awkward around her during the past few days, when they had always been so close, so connected, so easy together before. Passion was only a part of their relationship—though certainly a major part. But the mental connection between them was even more special—or at least it had been.

She didn't know what had gone wrong. Everything had seemed so perfect until Josh's behavior had suddenly changed. But maybe the questions he had asked her dad tonight had been a clue. Maybe he had concluded that he didn't really want to spend the rest of his life with her. That only a few men were lucky enough to find "the one."

She had so hoped she was Josh's "one."

Feeling tears threaten again, she drew a deep breath and lifted her chin, ordering herself to reclaim her pride. She would survive losing Josh, she assured herself. Maybe.

Forcing herself to leave Abby's guest bathroom, she headed for the dining room, expecting to hear conversation and the clinking of silverware and china. Instead what appeared to be stunned silence gripped the five people sitting at the table. Her gaze went instinctively to Josh, finding him staring back at her. His dark blond hair tumbled almost into his eyes, making him look oddly disheveled and perturbed. She realized suddenly that everyone else was gawking at her, too. Did she see sympathy on her father's face?

Before she could stop herself, she leaped to a stomach-wrenching conclusion. Had Josh told her family that he was breaking up with her? Is that why they were all looking at her like…well, like that?

"What?" she asked apprehensively.

"Why didn't you tell me?" Josh demanded.

It occurred to her that he sounded incongruously hurt, considering he was the one on the verge of breaking her heart. "Tell you what?"

"That you're pregnant."

"I'm—?" Her voice shot up into a squeak of surprise, unable to complete the sentence.

"Don't worry, darling, we'll all be here for you," Diana assured her, wiping her eyes with the corner of a napkin. "Just as we'll be here for you, Abby, after you and Greg split up. Although I sincerely hope you'll try to work everything out before you go your separate ways."

"Wait. What?" Greg's chair scraped against the floor as he spun to stare at his wife. "What is she talking about, Abby?"

Melissa felt as if she'd left a calm, orderly dinner party and returned only minutes later to sheer pandemonium.

"What on earth makes you think I'm pregnant?" she asked Josh, unable to concentrate on her sister's sputtering at the moment.

He looked from her to her mom and back again, growing visibly more confused by the minute. "Your mother told us."

Her mother sighed and nodded. "I've overheard a few snippets of conversation today. Enough to put two and two together about what's going on with both my poor girls. You're giving up caffeine and you're feeling queasy and we've all noticed that you've been upset all evening."

"Mom, I don't know what you heard—" Abby began, but Melissa talked over her sister.

"You're completely off base, Mom," she said firmly, avoiding Josh's eyes until she was sure she could look at him without succumbing to those looming tears again. "I'm giving up caffeine because I think I've been drinking too much of it for my health. I'm not pregnant."

Regret swept through her with the words. Maybe she was being overly dramatic again, but the thought of never having a child with Josh almost sent her bolting for the bathroom with another bout of hot tears.

She risked a quick glance at him, but she couldn't quite read his expression. He sat silently in his chair, his expression completely inscrutable now. She assumed he was deeply relieved to find out she wasn't pregnant, but the relief wasn't evident on his face. Maybe he was thinking about what a close call he'd just escaped.

Her mom searched her face. "You're not?"

Melissa shook her head. "No. I'm not."

"Then why have you been so upset this evening?"

Rattled by this entire confrontation, she blurted, "I'm upset because Josh is breaking up with me."

Josh made a choked sound before pushing a hand through his hair in exasperation. "Why do you think I'm breaking up with you?"

"I just, um, put two and two together," she muttered, all too aware that she sounded as much like her mother as Abby always accused her.

"Well, then you need to work on your math skills," Josh shot back with a frustrated shake of his head. "I don't want to break up with you, Melissa. I want to ask you to marry me!"

Chapter Six
by Cindy Kirk

Bedlam followed Josh Wright's announcement that he planned to propose to Melissa Morgan. Everyone at the table started talking in loud excited voices, their hands gesturing wildly.

Family patriarch Frank Morgan had experience with chaotic situations. After all, he and his wife Diana had raised two girls. When things got out of hand, control had to be established. Because his silver referee whistle was in a drawer back home, Frank improvised.

Seconds later, a shrill noise split the air.

His family immediately stopped talking and all turned in his direction.

"Frank?" Shock blanketed Greg DeSena's face.

Though he'd been married to Frank's oldest daughter, Abby, for three years, this was a side to his father-in-law he'd obviously never seen.

Frank's youngest daughter, Melissa, slipped into her chair without being asked. She cast furtive glances at her boyfriend, Josh. It had been Josh's unexpected proclamation that he intended to propose to her that had thrown everyone into such a tizzy.

Even though Frank hadn't whistled a family meeting to order in years, his wife and daughters remembered what the blast of air meant.

"Darling." Diana spoke in a low tone, but loud enough for everyone at the table to hear clearly. "This is our anniversary dinner. Can't a family meeting wait until another time?"

Her green eyes looked liked liquid jade in the candlelight. Even after thirty years, one look from her, one touch, was all it took to make Frank fall in love all over again.

If they were at their home—instead of at Greg and Abby's house—he'd grab her hand and they'd trip up the stairs, kissing and shedding clothes with every step. But he was the head of this warm, wonderful, sometimes crazy family and with the position came responsibility.

"I'm sorry, sweetheart. This can't wait." Frank shifted his gaze from his beautiful wife and settled it on the man who'd blurted out his intentions only moments before. "Josh."

His future son-in-law snapped to attention. "Sir."

Though Frank hadn't been a marine in a very

long time, Josh's response showed he'd retained his commanding presence. "Sounds like there's something you want to ask my daughter."

"Frank, no. Not now," Diana protested. "Not like this."

"Mr. Morgan is right." Josh pushed back his chair and stood. "There *is* something I want to ask Melissa. From the misunderstanding tonight, it appears I've already waited too long."

Frank nodded approvingly and sat back in his chair. He liked a decisive man. Josh would be a good addition to the family.

"If you want to wait—" Diana began.

Before she could finish, Frank leaned over and did what he'd wanted to do all night. He kissed her.

"Let the man say his piece," he murmured against her lips.

Diana shuddered. Her breathing hitched but predictably she opened her mouth. So he kissed her again. This time deeper, longer, until her eyes lost their focus, until she relaxed against his shoulder with a happy sigh.

Josh held out his hand to Melissa. His heart pounded so hard against his ribs, he felt almost faint. But he was going to do it. Now. Finally.

With a tremulous smile, Melissa placed her slender fingers in his. The lines that had furrowed her pretty brow the past couple of weeks disappeared. His heart clenched as he realized he'd been to blame for her distress. Well, he wouldn't delay a second longer. He promptly dropped to one knee.

"Melissa," Josh began then stopped when his voice broke. He glanced around the table. All eyes were on him, but no one dared to speak. Abby and Greg offered encouraging smiles. His future in-laws nodded approvingly.

His girlfriend's eyes never left his face. The love he saw shining in the emerald depths gave him courage to continue.

"When I first saw you at the office Christmas party, I was struck by your beauty. It wasn't until we began dating that I realized you are as beautiful inside as out."

Melissa blinked back tears. Josh hoped they were tears of happiness.

"This past year I've fallen deeper and deeper in love with you. I can't imagine my life without you in it. I want your face to be the last I see at night and the first I see every morning. I want to have children with you. I want to grow old with you. I promise I'll do everything in my power to make you happy."

He was rambling. Speaking from the heart to be sure, but rambling. For a second Josh wished he had the speech he'd tinkered with over the past couple of months with him now, the one with the pretty words and poetic phrases. But it was across the room in his jacket pocket and too late to be of help now.

Josh slipped a small box from his pocket and snapped open the lid. The diamond he'd seen circled in her bride's magazine was nestled inside. The large stone caught the light and sparkled with an impressive brilliance. "I love you more than I thought it was possible to love someone."

He'd told himself he wasn't going to say another word but surely a declaration of such magnitude couldn't be considered rambling.

Her lips curved upward and she expelled a happy sigh. "I love you, too."

Josh resisted the urge to jump to his feet and do a little home-plate dance. He reminded himself there would be plenty of time for celebration once the ring was on her finger.

With great care, Josh lifted the diamond from the black velvet. He was primed to slip it on when she pulled her hand back ever-so-slightly.

"Isn't there something you want to ask me?" Melissa whispered.

At first Josh couldn't figure out what she was referring to until he realized with sudden horror that he hadn't actually popped the question. Heat rose up his neck. Thankfully he was still on one knee. "Melissa, will you make me the happiest man in the world and marry me?"

The words came out in one breath and were a bit garbled, but she didn't appear to notice.

"Yes. Oh, yes."

Relief flooded him. He slid the ring in place with trembling fingers. "If you don't like it we can—"

"It's perfect. Absolutely perfect." Tears slipped down her cheeks.

He stood and pulled her close, kissing her soundly. "I wanted this to be special—"

"It is special." Melissa turned toward her family and smiled through happy tears. "I can't imagine anything better than having my family here to celebrate with us."

"This calls for a toast." Flashing a smile that was almost as bright as his daughter's, Frank picked up the nearest bottle of champagne. He filled Diana's glass and then his own before passing the bottle around the table.

Greg filled his glass and those of Josh and Melissa's but Abby, his wife, covered her glass with her hand and shook her head.

Frank stood and raised his glass high. "To Josh and Melissa. May you be as happy together as Diana and I have been for the past thirty years."

Words of congratulations and the sound of clinking glasses filled the air.

Nestled in the crook of her future husband's arm, Melissa giggled. Normally her mom knew everything before everyone else. Not this time.

"You thought I was pregnant because I wanted decaf coffee," she said to her mother, "but yet you don't find it odd that Abby hasn't had a sip of alcohol tonight?"

For a woman like Diana who prided herself on being in the "know," the comment was tantamount to waving a red flag in front of a bull. She whirled and fixed her gaze on her firstborn, who stood with her head resting against her husband's shoulder. "Honey, is there something you and Greg want to tell us?"

Abby's cheeks pinked. She straightened and exchanged a look with her husband. He gave a slight nod. She took one breath. And then another. "Greg and I, well, we're…we're pregnant."

"A baby!" Diana shrieked and moved so suddenly she'd have upset her glass of champagne, if Frank hadn't grabbed it. "I can't believe it. Our two girls, all grown up. One getting married. One having a baby. This is truly a happy day."

Everyone seemed to agree as tears of joy flowed as freely as the champagne, accompanied by much back-slapping.

"Have you thought of any names?" Diana asked Abby and Greg then turned to Melissa and Josh. "Any idea on a wedding date?"

Suggestions on both came fast and furious until Abby realized the party had gotten off track. She pulled her sister aside. "The anniversary gift," she said in a low tone to Melissa. "We need to give them their gift."

"I'll get it." In a matter of seconds, Melissa returned, cradling the large basket in her arms.

Josh moved to her side, as if he couldn't bear to be far from his new fiancée. Greg stood behind his wife, his arms around her still slender waist.

"Mom and Dad," Melissa began. "You've shown us what love looks like."

"What it feels like," Abby added.

With a flourish, Melissa presented her parents with a basket overflowing with biscotti, gourmet cappuccino mix, and other items reminiscent of their honeymoon in Italy…along with assorted travel documents. "Congratulations on thirty years of marriage."

"And best wishes for thirty more," Abby and Melissa said in unison, with Josh and Greg chiming in.

"Oh, Frank, isn't this the best evening ever?" Diana's voice bubbled with excitement. "All this good news and gifts, too."

She exclaimed over every item in the basket but grew silent when she got to the tickets, guidebooks and brochures. Diana glanced at her husband. He shrugged, looking equally puzzled.

"It's a trip," Abby explained.

Melissa smiled. "We've booked you on a four-star vacation to Italy, so you can recreate your honeymoon, only this time in comfort and style."

"Oh, my stars." Diana put a hand to her head. When she began to sway, her husband slipped a steadying arm around her shoulders.

"I think your mom has had a bit too much excitement for one day." Frank chuckled. "Or maybe a little too much of the vino."

"I've only had two glasses. Or was it three?" Instead of elbowing him in the side as he expected, she laughed and refocused on her children. "Regardless, thank you all for such wonderful, thoughtful presents."

Abby exchanged a relieved glance with Melissa. "We wanted to give you and Dad the perfect gift to celebrate your years of happiness together."

"You already have," Frank said, his voice thick with emotion.

He shifted his gaze from Abby and Greg to Melissa and Josh before letting it linger on his beautiful wife, Diana. A wedding in the spring. A grandbaby next summer. A wonderful woman to share his days and nights. Who could ask for more?

* * * * *

HEART & HOME

Heartwarming romances where love can
happen right when you least expect it.

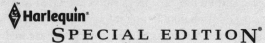

SPECIAL EDITION®

COMING NEXT MONTH
AVAILABLE APRIL 24, 2012

#2185 FORTUNE'S UNEXPECTED GROOM
The Fortunes of Texas: Whirlwind Romance
Nancy Robards Thompson

#2186 A DOCTOR IN HIS HOUSE
McKinley Medics
Lilian Darcy

**#2187 HOLDING OUT FOR DOCTOR
PERFECT**
Men of Mercy Medical
Teresa Southwick

**#2188 COURTED BY THE TEXAS
MILLIONAIRE**
St. Valentine, Texas
Crystal Green

#2189 MATCHMAKING BY MOONLIGHT
Teresa Hill

#2190 THE SURPRISE OF HER LIFE
Helen R. Myers

You can find more information on upcoming Harlequin® titles,
free excerpts and more at www.HarlequinInsideRomance.com.

HSECNM0412

REQUEST YOUR FREE BOOKS!
2 FREE NOVELS PLUS 2 FREE GIFTS!

SPECIAL EDITION
Life, Love & Family

YES! Please send me 2 FREE Harlequin® Special Edition novels and my 2 FREE gifts (gifts are worth about $10). After receiving them, if I don't wish to receive any more books, I can return the shipping statement marked "cancel." If I don't cancel, I will receive 6 brand-new novels every month and be billed just $4.49 per book in the U.S. or $5.24 per book in Canada. That's a saving of at least 14% off the cover price! It's quite a bargain! Shipping and handling is just 50¢ per book in the U.S. and 75¢ per book in Canada.* I understand that accepting the 2 free books and gifts places me under no obligation to buy anything. I can always return a shipment and cancel at any time. Even if I never buy another book, the two free books and gifts are mine to keep forever.

235/335 HDN FEGF

Name	(PLEASE PRINT)	
Address		Apt. #
City	State/Prov.	Zip/Postal Code

Signature (if under 18, a parent or guardian must sign)

Mail to the **Reader Service**:
IN U.S.A.: P.O. Box 1867, Buffalo, NY 14240-1867
IN CANADA: P.O. Box 609, Fort Erie, Ontario L2A 5X3

Not valid for current subscribers to Harlequin Special Edition books.

Want to try two free books from another line?
Call 1-800-873-8635 or visit www.ReaderService.com.

* Terms and prices subject to change without notice. Prices do not include applicable taxes. Sales tax applicable in N.Y. Canadian residents will be charged applicable taxes. Offer not valid in Quebec. This offer is limited to one order per household. All orders subject to credit approval. Credit or debit balances in a customer's account(s) may be offset by any other outstanding balance owed by or to the customer. Please allow 4 to 6 weeks for delivery. Offer available while quantities last.

Your Privacy—The Reader Service is committed to protecting your privacy. Our Privacy Policy is available online at www.ReaderService.com or upon request from the Reader Service.

We make a portion of our mailing list available to reputable third parties that offer products we believe may interest you. If you prefer that we not exchange your name with third parties, or if you wish to clarify or modify your communication preferences, please visit us at www.ReaderService.com/consumerschoice or write to us at Reader Service Preference Service, P.O. Box 9062, Buffalo, NY 14269. Include your complete name and address.

HSE11B

After a bad decision—or two—Annie Mendes is determined to succeed as a P.I. But her first assignment could be her last, because one thing is clear: she's not cut out to be a nanny. And Louisiana detective Nate Dufrene seems to know there's more to her than meets the eye!

Read on for an exciting excerpt of the upcoming book WATERS RUN DEEP by Liz Talley...

THE SOUND OF A CAR behind her had Annie scooting off the road and checking over her shoulder.

Nate Dufrene.

Her heart took on a galloping rhythm that had nothing to do with exercise.

He slowed beside her. "Wanna ride?"

"I'm almost there. Besides, I wouldn't want to get your seat sweaty."

His gaze traveled down her body before meeting her eyes. Awareness ignited in her blood. "I don't mind."

Her mind screamed, *get your butt back to the house and leave Nate alone.* Her libido, however, told her to take the candy he offered and climb into his car like a naughty little girl. Damn, it was hard to ignore candy like him.

"If you don't mind." She pulled open the door and climbed inside.

The slight scent of citrus cologne, which suited him, filled the car. She inhaled, sucking in cool air and Nate. Both were good.

"You run often?" he asked.

"Three or four times a week."

"Oh, yeah? Maybe we can go for a run together."

Her body tightened unwillingly as thoughts of other things they could do together flitted through her mind. She

HSREXP0412

shrugged as though his presence wasn't affecting her. Which it *so* was. Lord, what was wrong with her? *He* wasn't her assignment.

"Sure." No way—not if she wanted to keep her job. As he parked, she reached for the door handle, but his hand on her arm stopped her. His touch was warm, even on her heated flesh.

"What did you say you were before becoming a nanny?"

Alarm choked out the weird sexual energy that had been humming in her for the past few minutes. Maybe meeting him on the road wasn't as coincidental as it first seemed. "A real-estate agent."

Will Nate discover Annie's secret?
Find out in WATERS RUN DEEP by Liz Talley,
available May 2012 from Harlequin® Superromance®.

And be sure to look for the other two books
in Liz's THE BOYS OF BAYOU BRIDGE series,
available in July and September 2012.

HSREXP0412